WHO SO DETESTS THE DIETITIAN?

GAVIN LEBENHOM
An unpublished mystery writer who desperately wants to create the perfect mystery weekend?

REGGIE KNIGHT
The handsome Jamaican pop star who harbors a long-held grudge for a murderous deed?

NANCY LEBENHOM
The too-dutiful wife who would do almost anything for her ne'er-do-well husband?

SYBIL CLIFTON MONTROSE
The hostess *extraordinaire*, who is the only guest to know the unfortunate victim in his early, less careful days?

DOLORES CARTER-WHITE
The beautiful and famous romance writer, would she go to any lengths to protect her decidedly unglamorous past from her demanding, adoring public?

Also by E. X. Giroux
Published by Ballantine Books:

A DEATH FOR ADONIS

A DEATH FOR A DARLING

A DEATH FOR A DANCER

A DEATH FOR A DOCTOR

A DEATH FOR A DILETTANTE

A DEATH FOR A DIETITIAN

E. X. Giroux

BALLANTINE BOOKS • NEW YORK

Library of Congress Catalog Card Number: 87-28622

ISBN 0-345-35767-1

This edition published by arrangement with St. Martin's Press, Inc.

Manufactured in the United States of America

First Ballantine Books Edition: October 1989

For Margaret J. Henricks,
who shared many a Christmas past

CHAPTER ONE

Robert Forsythe cursed explosively and jabbed the bell connecting his desk with his secretary's. When Mrs. Sutter appeared, he transferred his glower from the brief before him to her placid face. "I asked for the Denton brief and you brought the Desston—"

"Mr. Forsythe, I could have sworn you meant the Desston one."

"I generally *mean* what I *say*. Kindly replace this and bring the correct one."

Hot color swept up her short neck, mantling the chipmunk cheeks of her no longer placid face. "It's not easy, you know, trying to replace Miss Sanderson. She has her own system, if you could call it that, and a right jumble it is. Everything helter-skelter—"

"It works for her." He thrust the folder out.

Without a word Mrs. Sutter seized it, spun on her heels, and stalked out. She didn't bother closing the door, and the barrister jumped up and pushed it to. Returning to the massive leather chair used in turn by his father and grandfather, he stared at the oaken panel. He had been harsh with his temporary secretary and the woman had a valid point. Not only did Sandy have her own mystifying system, but she

1

was a hard act for anyone to follow. Abigail Sanderson seemed to possess an amazing amount of ESP and quite often handed him the material he needed without waiting to be asked. Of course, Forsythe thought, Sandy was not only his secretary but had once been his father's. And she was much more than a good right hand in chambers. Following the death of his mother, Sandy had assumed the maternal duties for a three-year-old boy. Through the years she had been friend, confidant, and at times, a sharp and exasperating spur. How, he wondered, could he have expected poor Mrs. Sutter, at short notice, to step into shoes such as those. And why had he practically forced Sandy to take the entire month off? Perhaps he had suffered momentarily from an overdose of Christmas spirit. All she had asked for had been a couple of days to do her shopping.

"Take the rest of the month," he had urged.

"But Robby," she protested, "it's only the first of December."

"Decembers are generally slow."

"Not always. This one might be hectic."

"Nonsense, we won't even know you're gone." He added grandly, "Consider it a Christmas present."

"I'd rather settle for an emerald pendant. Something small but elegant."

"You're talking to a barrister, not an oil magnate. Now scoot before I change my mind."

She had scooted, but her prediction had started to come true. The next week had been a nightmare, with briefs flooding in and his juniors, clerks, and office staff trying vainly to cope. Shifting in his chair, Forsythe banged open a drawer. It looked as though there was going to be a delay in getting that damn brief. Might as well do some work on the one he was leading young Peters in. Spreading the leaves of the folder, he bent his narrow head over it. The door squeaked open, someone moved across the room, and

2

the Denton brief was slapped down over the one he was reading.

Without looking up he said, "Sorry I was so short, Mrs. Sutter—"

"What did you say to the poor thing, Robby? When I came in she was practically in tears."

"Sandy!" His head jerked up and he repeated with a rising inflection, "Sandy?"

"The new Abigail Sanderson." She pirouetted. "What do you think? And please close your mouth. You're managing to look like an idiot."

He closed his mouth but continued to stare. His Sandy had always been carefully groomed, with gray hair modishly styled, and the long lean body discreetly clothed in tailored suits and dresses. This Sandy. . .

She complacently patted her hair. Gray waves had been cropped into a cap of curls hugging a finely shaped head and, by some miracle of a hairdresser's art, turned a glossy silver. Makeup made her pale blue eyes look darker and discreetly softened the austere lines of her cheeks and chin. But that wasn't all. Layers of assorted shades of green chiffon wafted about her thin body. As far as Forsythe could tell, the layers began with apple-green and charged through the spectrum to a final emerald.

"What in God's name have you done to yourself?" he blurted.

"Come up to date and it's high time." She fingered a barbaric silver bracelet studded with what looked like chunks of jade. "And *I* didn't do it. This took time, energy, and an assortment of hairdresser and couturieres to accomplish. To say nothing of an appalling amount of money." She sat and crossed her legs, dangling a shapely limb covered with a mist of sea-green and ending in an emerald-shod foot. "Well? Do say what you think."

Her employer's mouth snapped open to do exactly that,

and then he decided discretion might be the best part of valor. "Takes a bit of getting used to," he said weakly. "Rather exotic, but yes . . . you do look quite nice."

"*Nice.*" Her lips curled. "You dote on quotes so here's one for you: 'It is a certain sign of mediocrity always to praise moderately.' As for you . . ." She critically eyed his dark suit, chalk-white shirt, and narrow striped tie. "Wouldn't hurt to change your own dull image. Here's a start." Picking up a parcel she had dropped on a chair near the door, she tossed it to him.

Paper rustled and he stared down at a hot pink shirt and a yellow and mauve ascot. "To measure up to these I'd have to have my hair tinted magenta and orange and buy a lavender velvet suit. Sandy, I'm a barrister, not a pimp."

She came out of her chair like a big green cat. "Are you implying I look like a hooker? And to think I was going to offer to come back and straighten things out here." In a swirl of chiffon she headed toward the door.

"Sandy!" He caught her arm. "Look, I'm abjectly sorry. You look wonderful, marvelous! I'll wear your gifts, I swear. It's simply I've never seen you looking so radiant, so—"

"Don't overdo it. You'll run out of adjectives." She smiled up at him and this was the gamine grin of the old Sandy. "Apology accepted. I'll even reconsider my intention of helping you out of this mess."

He was tempted to accept but successfully resisted. "Not necessary. We'll cope. Now, do sit down and tell me what your plans are for the remainder of the month."

"Ply me with drink and I'll tell all. Ah, whiskey. Not too much soda, Robby, I'm feeling rather festive." She took a long drink. "The day after tomorrow I leave for a remote island, or sort of island, where I will, unaided, solve the dastardly crime of murder. Rather stealing your thunder, eh?" She extended her glass. "Perhaps a touch more of your vintage stock."

He tilted the decanter over her glass. "I have a hunch you were imbibing whiskey, vintage or not, before you got here."

"Not so. I'm completely sober. On this sort of an island is a centuries-old inn filled with ghosts and brooding violence—"

"Just what is 'a sort of an island'?"

"A small chunk of land connected by a spur of land at low tide with the mainland. A sort of causeway. Are you, I hope, confused, barrister?"

"Not so," he echoed. "Sounds as though you've been invited to one of those murder parties that are so popular now. The ones where people spend enormous amounts of money to act out the plot of an ancient mystery novel."

"A modern one. Hot off the author's word processor." She waved airily and the bracelet glinted. "And my fellow guests will be celebrities, noted figures in the art world, and so on. And the celebrity sleuth will be none other than *moi*."

"Just how did they latch on to you, Sandy?"

"Slightly green-eyed, aren't you?"

"Certainly not."

"Well, somewhat disgruntled. To be truthful, you were the one they wanted, but they had to settle for me. As I explained, you'll be far too busy coping without me to—"

"I might have been able to arrange it."

"And that's why I haven't mentioned it before." Cool blue eyes examined him. "You're really getting hooked on this crime bit."

"You must admit the cases we've been involved with have been more exciting than receiving instruction from solicitors."

"*You* have been involved with. All I've ever done is trail

5

along and make notes and let you bang ideas off me."

It was his turn to look searchingly at his secretary. "You did a first-rate job all on your own in Maddersley."

She said wryly, "And managed to get nearly killed because I couldn't figure out who had butchered that family. But this will be different. All playacting and fun and games."

The telephone shrilled and he lifted it. "I'm busy, Mrs. Sutter. Well . . . ask Vincent to handle it. No further calls, please. And Mrs. Sutter, sorry I was so abrupt earlier." Replacing the receiver, he said firmly, "Stop tantalizing and tell all."

"To do that I'd have to go back to my school days."

"The condensed version."

She settled back in her chair. "During those school days my best friend was Peggy Green. An awfully nice girl, gentle and loyal and affectionate. Peggy married young, and I was horribly jealous when I met her fiancé. Not only was Noel Canard a naval officer, but he was incredibly handsome. Looked exactly like my film idol of the time— Tyrone Power. I was Peggy's maid of honor and must confess spent most of the ceremony mooning over Noel. It wasn't long before I stopped mooning and decided better Peggy than me. Noel was as vain and selfish as he was handsome. After a time Peggy and I lost track of each other except for cards at Christmas and a birth announcement when their daughter, Nancy, was born. Then, last year . . ."

"Yes," Forsythe said gently. "I remember your attending Mrs. Canard's funeral. You mentioned her husband had died some years prior to your friend's death."

"And I wept all over your shoulder. Sheer guilt for not keeping in touch with Peggy. Of course Nancy was at her mother's funeral, and we spoke briefly. She told me about her father's death and also what had happened to him some years before it. There had been a fire aboard his ship and Noel was badly burned. Horribly disfigured, Nancy said. At the time the girl was fifteen, and after the accident she never saw her father again. And she rarely saw her mother. That's what I meant about Noel's being selfish. Nancy was bundled off to school and spent her vacations with relatives and friends."

"A grim life for a child," Forsythe said. "What about her mother?"

"Twice a year Peggy would come to London and visit her daughter, but the rest of the time she was holed up on that island I mentioned. Peggy's aunt owned the island and ran the inn there for years. Apparently at one time there was a fishing village on the mainland and the inn's clientele was drawn from there. Anyway, the aunt willed both inn and island to Peggy, and after Noel's release from the hospital, he insisted they live there." Miss Sanderson paused and then muttered, "It must have been a ghastly life. The only people on the island with them were an elderly couple who did the work. Noel wouldn't let them or even his wife see his face. Nancy said he wore some kind of mask."

"When did he die?"

"Five years ago. Either by accident or suicide. Noel tried to cross the rock causeway and was swept away by the incoming tide. His body was never found. For the first time Nancy went to the inn to persuade her mother to leave the place, to come to London and live with her. Peggy refused. She said her health was not good and she'd prefer to spend the short time left to her where she had lived so many years with Noel. Peggy was obsessively devoted to her husband."

"She must have been to desert her daughter like that." Forsythe shook a baffled head. "I take it the daughter,

Nancy Canard, is the one who invited you to the celebrity murder party."

"Nancy Lebonhom now. Recently she looked me up. She's married to a writer—Gavin Lebonhom—"

"The name doesn't ring a bell."

"For a good reason. Gavin hasn't published as yet. Nancy says that's the reason for turning the old inn into— what would you call it?"

Forsythe shrugged. "A money-making murder house?"

"Close enough. Not only should they have gobs of money from guests, but Gavin is convinced after the publicity on this first party publishers will be beating a path to his door, begging for scripts. Nancy says he's been working for weeks on the mystery script for this party. Everyone but the detective will have a script with dialogue and movements and so on. The great detective will ad-lib and guess the identity of the murderer. Finally"—she made an extravagant gesture—"I will have my very own case. Abigail Sanderson's first case!" She held out her glass. "On that note I will have a stirrup cup and take my leave."

Forsythe pushed the stopper into the neck of the decanter. "The bar is closed. I am not having you reel through chambers convincing the staff we've been closeted getting stinking. I must consider morale. They're probably still in shock over your new image."

She snorted. "Nervous Nellie nearly keeled over."

"Stop calling young Peters that, Sandy. Although, admittedly, it does fit. But it doesn't take much to shake Peters."

"About the only thing that would shake Vincent is an earthquake, and his mouth was sagging open even farther than yours did."

"By the way, what are the names of your fellow guests?"

"Haven't the foggiest. Nancy wants to surprise me."

She stood up and smoothed down chiffon. "Do you think I'll measure up?"

"Sandy, I promise you won't be overlooked no matter how scintillating your fellow guests. Have fun, but do keep in mind Christmas is being celebrated at the family house in Sussex and I'm counting on you for hostess duties."

She opened the door and struck a pose. "I shall be there though hell should bar the way."

"If you need help detecting," he said wistfully, "give me a ring."

"Find your own murder. Now, I go to solve heinous crimes, battle ghosts and things that go bong in the night. I go!" And in a swirl of multicolored chiffon, she went.

Forsythe tried to engross himself in the Denton brief, but his thoughts wandered back to his secretary. Ghosts, he thought, and one of them might be wearing a mask.

CHAPTER TWO

MISS SANDERSON'S MG WAS THE SAME SHADE AS THE final flimsy layer on her exotic new gown. But on this blustery afternoon she was sensibly attired in more prosaic clothing. The silver curls were concealed by a scarf, and chiffon had given place to wool trousers, a heavy pullover, and a jacket. As the small car darted over the dips and through the hollows of the narrow road, she gazed at the bleak countryside beyond the bare tangles of hedgerows. In summertime it might have had its own charm, but at present it was dreary, stretching away in monotones broken only by occasional copses of skeletal maples and alders. The only sign of life for miles was a huddle of sheep munching stolidly at browning grass.

She shivered, turned up the heater a notch, and glanced at the rearview mirror. At least she wasn't alone in this godforsaken country. The scarlet car still drifted along in her wake. It was closer than it had been, and she was now able to discern its make. A Lagonda. A fellow guest, she surmised. There was no other explanation for anyone's taking this road but for that reason. Then she grinned. Detecting already. Hedgerows dwindled and trailed off as the road widened into a graveled area. The sea was directly ahead, a heaving, leaden mass the same hue as the lowering clouds. On the gravel surface three vehicles were drawn up in a line, and beyond them a stone pier pointed like an accusing finger at a low-lying mass that had to be her destination. Pulling the car to a halt, she hopped out. The island was larger than she had expected and close enough that she could distinguish a sprawling structure and something that looked like a boathouse. She had half expected to find a boat waiting on this side, but there was nothing but the lonely pier, the sky, and water. Well, at least some company was arriving. The fiery red Lagonda drew up smartly, and its sole occupant got out.

Miss Sanderson took one look and fought to control her expression. If she wasn't careful, she would be gaping with the same idiotic look that Robby had turned on her a couple of days ago. She had never seen the Lagonda's driver in the flesh, but that face had looked up at her from the sleeves of the albums she had purchased as Christmas gifts for two teenaged nieces. The clerk had assured her that this pop star was the current rage and her nieces would be ecstatic. Miss Sanderson had little knowledge of current rages and practically none about pop stars in general and had taken the clerk's word for it. On the record sleeve a golden-skinned person, attired in what looked like silk pajamas, reclined against a pile of satin pillows. Glossy black ringlets fell to silken shoulders, and from one earlobe a jeweled earring dangled. She couldn't decide whether the reclining figure was male or female. The face framed in ringlets was beautiful but completely androgynous. Any doubts were now laid to rest. He was beautiful but definitely male. The ringlets were topped by a knitted toque, the slender frame was attired in jeans and a white parka, and neither ear was adorned.

A hand was extended and his voice was melodious. "Reggie Knight," he told her. "And you are . . ."

11

She struggled for composure. If she wasn't careful, she would be begging for an autograph. "Abigail Sanderson. And you . . . you're the Black Knight."

White teeth flashed in a grin. "And you're Robert Forsythe's secretary." He glanced back at the narrow road. "Is he driving down by himself?"

"No. Robby is too busy to come. I'm substituting for him."

"That ruddy Felix! All but swore on the Bible that Forsythe would be here."

"Sorry. You'll have to settle for me."

Turning away abruptly, Knight stared out over the sea. "The only reason I'm here is because of Forsythe. Damn it to hell!"

Drawing herself up, Miss Sanderson said tartly, "I said I was sorry."

The beautiful face was suddenly contrite. "And I'm sorry too. Sorry I snapped at you like that. Put it down to artistic temperament." He turned up his collar and the white material contrasted as startlingly with the dark features as the flash of teeth had. "No sign of life on the island. Think they're going to leave us here to freeze?"

"I'm halfway there already." She glanced at the other cars. There was an elegant black Rolls, a white Cadillac, and a shabby brown Mini. "Looks as though some guests have already arrived. Are you acquainted with any of them?"

He pointed at the Rolls. "Only Felix and Alice Caspari."

"Caspari. Hmm . . . that rings a bell. Didn't he have a show on television a while back? Got it! Felix Caspari, the cook."

Flinging back his head, the Black Knight roared with laughter. "*Cook*. How I wish you'd said that to Felix."

"Well . . . a chef, then."

"Felix prides himself on being modest. As he will soon

tell you, quite modestly, Felix Caspari is the chefs' chef. The gourmet genius whom master chefs turn to for advice."

"And Alice?"

His mirth faded. "Every genius requires a victim. Let's get out of this wind." He opened the door of the Lagonda. "I'll switch the motor on and at least we'll be warm."

Eagerly she crawled into the luxurious car. Soon the motor was purring and delicious warmth flooded out. She loosened her head scarf and unbuttoned her jacket. Her companion still huddled in his parka, rubbing his hands together. "Should have worn gloves. We Jamaicans feel the cold."

"You came from Jamaica?"

"My parents did. I'm a Liverpudlian. Ever been in Liverpool?"

"I've passed through."

"Wise thing to do. My happiest moment was when I left the place."

"You've come a long way."

"Riding the crest at present. Which means next week I may be a has-been. Pop stars have short professional lives."

"Some don't. Look at the Beatles."

He threw up his hands. "I *knew* you were going to say that. Name some others who are still popular."

"I'm afraid, Mr. Knight—"

"Reggie, please."

"Abigail, then. As I started to say, I know little about your field."

"Ah, but you know a great deal about your own." Opening the glove compartment, he pulled out a handsome silver flask. "Care for a nip?"

"Don't mind if I do." He poured into the silver cup that acted as a cap and handed it to her. As he lifted the flask to his lips, she studied his profile. Truly a beautiful lad, and perhaps that beauty would prolong his professional life. He seemed bitterly disappointed that Robby wasn't here. She probed a bit. "My profession, if you could call it that, is legal secretary to a barrister. Rather dull, don't you think?"

"That's only part of the story. The other, exciting part is being assistant to a man who has solved several affairs that the newspapers call 'impossible crimes.'" He quoted, "'Robert Forsythe, ably assisted by his secretary, Abigail Sanderson—'"

"Assisted," she said sharply. "A bumbling Watson."

"You sound resentful."

She was about to make a hot denial and then she said slowly, "I suppose, in a way, I am. Oh, not of Robby, but perhaps of his uncanny ability to take threads and knit them together. In every case I've had access to the same facts as he, and yet . . ."

"Forsythe puts them together and finds a solution and all you have are jigsaw pieces."

"Exactly. Afterward I always kick myself for not seeing it too."

He was gazing through the windshield at the island. "I'm interested in one particular case. I believe it was one of your earlier ones. Forsythe found the solution to a murder that had been committed many years before. Do you remember the one?"

"Vividly. It was our first case. And Robby solved it twenty-five years after the murder had been committed. It involved the Calvert family." She handed back the silver cup. "You're interested in vintage murders?"

"Not a murder . . . or maybe in a way it was." He swung around to face her. "Wouldn't you call the destruction of a name and a reputation a murderous deed?"

"It depends on the details—" She leaned forward. "Look. Signs of life. We're about to be rescued."

14

Switching off the ignition, he opened his door. "About time, Abigail."

They watched a figure on the island trotting down the path that led to the boathouse, and Miss Sanderson thought longingly of central heating, a good stiff drink, and a hot tub. Nancy Lebonhom had mentioned that her husband and she were looking forward to hosting parties for wealthy crime buffs, and the ancient inn had been renovated with this object in view.

The door of the boathouse opened and a trim speedboat nosed out. Behind the wheel was a figure muffled in what looked like a navy pea jacket, and behind the head strands of hair blew backward like a horse's tail. "That certainly isn't Nancy Lebonhom," she told Reggie.

"Felix mentioned you are a relative of our hostess. An aunt?"

"The chef was mistaken. I was a friend of Nancy's mother."

"Might better get out the luggage." While Miss Sanderson got her bag from her car, he lifted a case from the rear of the Lagonda. Carrying both bags, he strode toward the pier. "Ship ahoy," he shouted as the boat nudged the stone pier. "We were afraid we were going to be marooned here."

The woman leapt from the cockpit and tied the rope to a stanchion. "I should have kept a closer watch on shore," she told them as she loped up the pier. "Only noticed you moments ago. Welcome to the Jester."

She was as tall as Miss Sanderson and appeared to have much the same build. She was younger, looking in her thirties. Light brown hair was strained back from a long narrow face and secured with a leather shoelace. Her brown eyes were warm and intelligent. "Miss Sanderson and Mr. Knight. I'm Fran Hornblower."

"A good name for a mariner," Miss Sanderson told her,

and wondered if she should recognize the name. "Another guest?"

"A lowly retainer. A Jacqueline-of-all-trades."

"But Nancy said both her mother's employees were elderly."

"Too old to carry on. Peggy—Mrs. Canard—hired Hielkje and me when they retired. We've been here nearly two years. Hielkje is cook and housekeeper."

Reggie gave her his flashing smile. "And you're the handyman? Or should I say handywoman? Perhaps handyperson."

She smiled back. "Whatever, and much needed around the Jester."

"Is that the name of the island?"

"The inn. The island is nameless or was until recently. Gavin is now calling it Lebonhom Island."

"It's not actually an island, is it? Felix mentioned it has a connection with the mainland."

"Right at present it's high tide and the causeway is under several feet of water. It's not safe to use anyway. Quite rough and overgrown with mosses and lichens."

Miss Sanderson said, "Nancy told me the fishermen once used the causeway to get to the inn."

"Years ago, and it must have been in better shape then. There's no one left in the village now except an occasional transient. The cottages, like the inn, are built of stone and are still intact, but it's a ghost village. From the water you'll see it. And speaking of water, let's get underway. I imagine you're chilled."

"Clear through," Reggie told her. He waited until Fran was behind the wheel, and then he handed the cases down and helped Miss Sanderson into the boat. He unwound the rope and climbed down beside the secretary. The boat swooped around in a graceful curve and headed away from the pier. Fran waved a hand. "There's the village."

The cluster of stone cottages did look intact and so did their slate roofs. Reggie pointed. "Look. Smoke coming from a chimney. See? That house at the end of the street."

Fran shrugged. "Probably one of those transients I mentioned. Squatting for a couple of nights."

Miss Sanderson only glanced at the village. Her attention was on the inn. As they drew closer, she said, "It's much larger than I had pictured it, Fran."

"Gavin had that wing built on recently. Plans eventually to stick a matching one on the other side. His plans tend to be a bit grandiose."

"And you stayed on here after Peggy's death?"

"Nancy asked Hielkje and me to caretake until she was able to sell the place. But she married Gavin and he got a brainstorm going and decided to make his fortune here. Then they *really* needed us."

"Don't you find it lonely?" Reggie asked.

"I find it ideal."

Miss Sanderson huddled into her jacket. To take her mind off the cold she examined what she could see of the island. It didn't look ideal to her. A barren chunk of rock lunged out of the sea, and it was broken only by a few stunted trees and the sprawling building. The original inn was built of stone and was three-storied. Along the north side was a long addition in white clapboard, a single story. The recently added wing blended in surprisingly well with the inn. Small windows in both structures were bordered by black-painted shutters, and the only touch of color were red-tiled roofs. Fran expertly nudged the boat in against another stone pier, and in moments Miss Sanderson was following Fran up the steep path.

"It will be good to feel that central heating," Miss Sanderson said.

The brown ponytail bobbed as the woman turned to cast

a sharp look at Miss Sanderson. "Exactly what did Nancy tell you about the Jester?"

"That it's been completely modernized."

"Hardly. I better warn you. No central heating, no electricity, no—"

"What?" Reggie gave an anguished howl. "And that bloody Felix lured me down to a primitive hovel without even indoor plumbing!"

"You and a number of others." Fran was laughing and her eyes danced. "There *is* indoor plumbing and that's about it. Gavin didn't waste money on nonessentials like comfort. Put every pound he could borrow into paneling and antique furnishings. Atmosphere, he claims, is most important. When the money comes flooding in, he hopes to add heat and light."

"But how do you manage?" Miss Sanderson asked.

"That's why the Lebonhoms need me. There's a cookstove in the kitchen, an old gas refrigerator, a few kerosene heaters, kerosene lamps—"

"Heat?" Reggie wailed.

"Fireplaces that require enormous amounts of coal hauled in to them."

Reggie had halted and now he lifted a fist and shook it in the direction of the inn. "I," he said decisively, "am going to kill that chefs' chef. I am going to carve him up with one of his custom-made knives."

"And I," Fran said heartily, "am more than willing to help you."

CHAPTER THREE

OVER THE INN DOOR A WEATHER-BEATEN BOARD CLAT-
tered in the wind. On it a capped and belled jester in faded
tints disported. On the other side of that door the lobby
spread out. Beside an oak desk was a door, a hall ran back
into the inn's depths, and on the far side was a set of tall
double doors. The lobby was floored in red and black tiles,
and, rather charmingly, the red squares contained white-
painted chess pieces, the black tiles, red ones. A red phone
was perched on the desk, flanked by foot-high glass figures
of the red and white queens. Miss Sanderson's first impression was that the lobby wasn't much warmer than it
had been outside.

Fran Hornblower took Miss Sanderson's jacket and
Reggie's parka and toque and hung them on brass pegs
near the outer door. The other pegs were already crowded
with an assortment of raincoats, parkas, one lustrous dark
mink, and a short white fox cape. "Nancy," she called.
"Your guests are here."

One of the double doors was thrown open and a chunky
man popped out. Both his hands were outstretched and he
was beaming. "Your host, Gavin Lebonhom," Fran said.
"Gavin, this—"

"No need for introductions," he told them jovially. "Auntie Abby and the Black Knight. Welcome to Lebonhom Island and the Jester!"

"Reggie," the Black Knight said firmly.

"Abigail," Miss Sanderson said just as firmly.

"Righto. But Nan always calls you Auntie Abby."

"I prefer Abigail."

She did. Nancy Lebonhom was young enough that the auntie didn't jar, but her husband didn't appear to be much younger than Miss Sanderson. His thick dark hair was liberally salted with gray, and his upper lip was hidden under a salt-and-pepper waterfall mustache.

Shivering, Reggie clasped both arms over his chest. "Where's Felix?"

Their host raised a bushy brow. "Fran?"

"When I left he was in the kitchen venting his spleen on Alice and Hielkje."

"Tell him Abigail and Reggie have arrived and round up everyone for grog."

She shook her head and the ponytail bobbed. "I'm off on fuel detail. Those bedrooms are frigid. However, if you'd like to lug in coal, I'd be happy to oblige."

"You brought in fuel this morning. At least, every time I needed you that was your excuse."

"Any idea how much coal is needed to keep this place habitable, Gavin?"

"Very well, but if you see Nancy, tell her to bring the others." He took Miss Sanderson's arm. "Come into the bar and I'll stir up that grog and get you thawed out."

"That," Reggie told him, "will take some doing."

Gavin led them into the bar. "At one time this was the public bar. Saloon bar is back there. As much as possible I left it as it was when this place was actually used as an inn."

"Atmosphere," Reggie said.

20

"Precisely."

"I like it," Miss Sanderson said, looking around with delight. She felt as though she had stepped back in time. Here were the rough dark beams, the old oaken paneling, the wide polished counter, and the gleaming taps of an earlier century. In an alcove a stone-faced fireplace beamed heat. Spaced around the room were rustic tables and benches.

Reggie stretched like a cat and regarded their host more kindly. "Do those taps work?"

"Best of ale comes foaming out. But wouldn't you prefer grog?"

"Seldom drink anything stronger than beer. I can handle it myself. Put in a stint as a bartender at one time."

"As you wish. Abigail, come into the inglenook and I'll see what I can do for you."

The alcove was more a small room than the traditional inglenook. Cushioned benches almost ringed it, allowing only a narrow passageway to reach the outer room. Sinking on a bench, she stretched out her feet to the welcome heat and watched Gavin as he deftly mixed ingredients in a long-handled copper pot. "Did you ever put in a stint as a bartender?" she asked.

The waterfall mustache quivered as he smiled. "No, but I'm good with grog. Even Fran admits that, and she doesn't hand me compliments often. Simply can't understand a man who shuns manual labor. Ah, that should do it." He poured seething liquid into a pottery mug. "Careful, that's hot."

She inhaled the fumes and took a cautious sip. "Good! Nancy tells me you write."

"Been scribbling away for years with no result. Publishers are wary of taking a chance on an unknown writer. But I'm hopeful soon—" He broke off and bobbed to his feet. "Mrs. Montrose! Now, you probably recognize Reg-

21

gie Knight, and here is Abigail Sanderson. Abigail and Reggie, may I present Sybil Clifton Montrose."

Swinging around, Miss Sanderson saw a short, wiry woman leaning across the counter, gathering one of Reggie's hands in both of hers. "What a pleasure! To think the Black Knight is right here. I've all your records and—"

"Care for a beer, Mrs. Montrose?" Freeing his hand from her grasp, Reggie reached for a pewter tankard.

"Thanks, but no. I prefer grog. I've so many questions to ask you I hardly know where to begin. . . ."

Mrs. Montrose proceeded to ask questions and patiently the Black Knight answered them. While Gavin mixed hot water, whiskey, lemon, and sugar, Miss Sanderson studied the latest celebrity. Sybil Clifton Montrose, hostess *extraordinaire*, giver of parties and dinners that even the famous thirsted to attend. The photographs in magazines had been kind to her. In person she looked like an aging simian. Above a clever monkey face was a fluff of fine gray hair, and she wore gray slacks and a gray sweater, a padded red vest, and red sandals. The gray-and-red was echoed in a huge fluffy gray Persian with a red leather harness and leash linking it to its owner.

Reggie was drawing another beer and gazing, rather desperately, over Mrs. Montrose at Miss Sanderson. "Abigail," he called. "Do come and meet Mrs. Montrose."

As the secretary approached, the monkey face swung toward her. Mrs. Montrose's nostrils flared as though she had just caught scent of dead fish. Bright black eyes swept from Miss Sanderson's sturdy shoes to her silver curls. "Where is your employer?" she demanded.

"Robby wasn't able to come, Mrs.—"

"How disgusting!"

The older woman turned back to Reggie, and Miss Sanderson was left staring at her back. Hot color flooded into her face and she thought wrathfully: Disgusting is right, Mrs. Montrose, what a disgusting old witch you turn out to be.

"Allow me to explain, dear lady," Gavin said, and brushed by the secretary. He was practically babbling. "We did think Mr. Forsythe could make it, but at the last moment . . ."

Putting down his tankard, Reggie winked at Miss Sanderson and lifted the flap in the counter. "Come have a look at this, Abigail."

The "this" he was pointing at proved to be a framed watercolor on the wall between two windows. In Miss Sanderson's ear he hissed, "A rude old girl, isn't she?"

"Obviously has no time for anyone but celebrities," she said tartly. "Hmm, that picture is charming."

"Think so? Take a closer look."

She took a closer look. It *was* charming. Three children, two girls and a boy, were skating on a frozen pond. The boy was falling, and the little girls, mittened hands clasped, were skating past him, tiny faces rosy and laughing. The pond was ringed by bushes and tall evergreens towering against a bright sky. Then she saw it. Behind a bush, merging with the shadows of the trees, was another, darker shadow. Something misshapen, menacing, a feeling of malevolence. Innocence threatened by evil. She whispered, "What's that he—it—is holding?"

"At a guess I'd say an ax."

"Blimey!" She stood to one side and studied the scene. "Couldn't it be an optical illusion, the play of light and shadow? It's not all that distinct."

Lustrous ringlets shook. "Looks deliberate. Like a maniac about to use an ax on those kids. Wonder who painted it?" Swinging around, he called, "Gavin, who is the artist?"

Their host, who had been hovering over an irate Mrs. Montrose, looked relieved and hurried over. "My wife's

23

father. Abigail, I understand you knew Noel Canard."

"For a brief time, long ago. I didn't know he painted."

"Nancy said her father had his heart set on an art career, but his family forced him into the navy. He did most of his painting after the accident. I've pieces of his work in all the guest rooms."

"Atmosphere?" Reggie asked.

"They do help." Fondly, Gavin regarded the watercolor. "A waste of talent, wasn't it? In the navy when he should have been—"

"Where is my grog?" Mrs. Montrose snapped.

"Coming right up."

Reggie watched the other man steering Mrs. Montrose to the alcove and said caustically, "He's lived with that horror and hasn't even seen it. Some atmosphere and some writer!"

Miss Sanderson dragged her eyes away from the picture. "I doubt I would have if you hadn't called my attention to it."

"Oh, *you* would have seen it."

Mrs. Montrose, now huddling near the fire, demanded, "Just where is Felix? I want a word with him."

"Yes," Reggie said. "Where is that bloody Felix?"

"Did someone mention my name?" a deep voice asked from the direction of the double doors.

Reggie strode forward. "Hiding, weren't you? Skulking around waiting for me to cool down."

"I rarely skulk. I've been working my fingers to the bone in that excuse for a kitchen, preparing a suitable dinner for all you lovely people. Gavin! Why haven't you done something about that primitive hole? How do you expect haute cuisine to appear from a nineteenth-century dungeon?"

An unbecoming flush mottled Gavin Lebonhom's face. "You know perfectly well the funds wouldn't stretch that far. Not after fixing up that VIP suite for you."

Reggie clamped a rough hand on Felix's shoulder. "Don't try to change the subject. You lied to both Mrs. Montrose and me. Assured us that Robert Forsythe would be here."

Felix sketched a cross over his creamy Aran sweater. "Only repeated what I'd been told. Nancy assured me that—"

"Like hell I did!" Nancy Lebonhom had entered the bar. "I told you what Auntie Abby said—Auntie Abby, you're finally here!" The girl rushed to embrace the older woman. "I'm so happy to see you!"

"You appear to be in the minority, Nancy." Fondly, Miss Sanderson gazed down at the round face, the short honey curls, the luminous hazel eyes. Nancy looked so much like her mother had at the same age.

Felix Caspari was trying to break loose from the Black Knight's golden hands. "Unhand me and let bygones be bygones. After all, we're gathered together for fun and games." He added plaintively, "Be a good chap and let me welcome Abigail." Reggie's hands fell away and Felix hastily walked over to Nancy and Miss Sanderson. "Despite this misunderstanding, I'm certain we are all delighted to meet you."

"I feel about as welcome as an outbreak of measles at a boarding school," Miss Sanderson told him bleakly.

"Then we'll have to make amends, won't we." Felix struck a pose. He was a handsome man. Tall and well built with a mane of chestnut hair, a short-cropped beard, sensual lips parted in a wide smile, shrewd eyes that weren't smiling. "I feel no need to introduce myself."

"Yes," Miss Sanderson said demurely. "I've heard about you. You're a cook."

Reggie made a sound much like the crow of a rooster and Felix gave a strangled one that sounded remarkably like a growl. "Dear Abigail, I am the chef's chef, consulted by master chefs the world over. Although I am a modest man and often refer to myself as a dietitian—"

"Felix was never trained as a chef," Mrs. Montrose announced acidly. She had left the alcove and was leading her cat toward the counter. "The closest he came to it was the dietitian course I arranged for him when he was a young chap."

"Sybil," Felix confided to Miss Sanderson, "is my very dear friend."

"Patron," that lady corrected. "Felix's grandfather was our gardener, and Felix grew up as playmate to my son."

"Patron and friend," Felix said smoothly. "And the good angel who funded a catering business for me and sponsored me so I was able to get my start."

"At a price," a light female voice said.

Two women had entered the room from the saloon bar. The one who had spoken was in the lead. She was a small dowdy woman, possessed of a faded prettiness. In one hand she clasped a large tapestry knitting bag.

Thumping her mug on the bar, Mrs. Montrose told Miss Sanderson, "This is the cook's wife, Alice Caspari. And dear Alice, as *you* should know, everyone has a price."

Miss Sanderson was paying little attention. Mrs. Montrose had mentioned a son. Recently she had heard or read about that son. Yes, now she remembered, and a feeling of compassion for the elderly woman stirred. For years that son had been comatose, hooked up to a life-support system. After a great deal of effort his mother had won the legal battle and the life supports had been removed, the poor man allowed to die.

Miss Sanderson was polite to Alice Caspari and accepted a large flabby hand belonging to the tall woman who had accompanied the chef's wife.

"I might better introduce myself. No one else will bother. Hielkje Visser."

"Dutch?" Miss Sanderson asked.

"Frisian."

"Isn't Friesland a province of the Netherlands?"

"A true Frisian would hotly debate that, but as a half-Frisian—my mother was English—I'll answer yes."

"And you looked after Peggy Canard."

"Fran and I. We grew very fond of her. Peggy was a kind lady."

"Nancy is the picture of her mother, Hielkje."

"Perhaps when Peggy was young. When I met her, she had snow-white hair and was most frail. But yes, Nancy's eyes are like Peggy's were. Same color and as bright. You were Peggy's friend?"

"School friend. After Peggy's marriage we drifted apart."

"That happens." Hielkje gave a heavy sigh.

"I was wondering, Hielkje, if you would be kind enough to point me toward my room."

"You've had your fill of celebrities?"

"Completely sated, and I'd also like to freshen up."

"I'll check with Fran. She's trying to take the chill off some of the guest rooms."

Leaning against the edge of a long table, Miss Sanderson eyed the woman's broad back. Hielkje Visser was heavyset and her walk was brisk, but her skin had a yellowish tinge and purplish pouches sagged under her brown eyes. She looked far from healthy. Miss Sanderson retreated to the alcove and found the little room unoccupied. She sank down near the hearth and rested her chin on a hand. She was gazing into the flames when she felt something soft brushing against her leg. It was the gray Persian, its smoky eyes glinting in the firelight. Bending,

27

she rubbed the animal behind an ear. It arched its back and broke into a husky purr.

"Omar likes you, Abigail." Mrs. Montrose sank down beside the secretary. "An honor. He seldom takes to anyone. I feel I should . . . I really wasn't very nice to you earlier, was I?"

"No."

"In fact I was curt. I fear I don't take disappointment well, but I shouldn't have taken it out on you. As I grow older I seem to be getting more querulous." One monkey claw patted Miss Sanderson's knee. "Shall we start afresh?"

Lifting her eyes, Miss Sanderson saw the wrinkled face so close to her own lighted with a warm and engaging smile. She had been wondering how this irascible old woman had ever managed to become a sought-after hostess. Now she could see Sybil Montrose had two sides. This one was all warmth and charm, and Miss Sanderson warily wondered if Mrs. Montrose might have an ulterior purpose.

Omar left off purring and jerked away from the secretary's hand, giving vent to a loud and menacing hiss. Reggie Knight, carrying a foaming tankard, circled the cat and sat down opposite the two women. He told Omar's mistress, "I can see why you keep that animal leashed. Looks positively fierce."

She turned her smile on him. "What you're thinking is like pet, like owner. I was just apologizing to Abigail for my foul temper. Come to mama, darling." Scooping up the cat, she settled it on her lap and ran a soothing hand down the silky back. "When I get back to London, I'm planning a dinner party and I'm so hoping to have all of you there."

Reggie shook his dark head. "I seldom go to social deals."

28

"I've heard that. Which is why I was so anxious to meet you and Dolly and Mr. Forsythe—"

"Dolly?"

"You and Abigail haven't met her yet. She's spent most of the afternoon in her room. Said she had some work to do on her latest book."

"Another writer?"

"This time a famous one." The cat flexed claws against Mrs. Montrose's knee and she winced. "Don't do that, Omar! He has the worst habits. When he's happy he practically claws one raw. As I started to say, Reggie, the three of you are such retiring people it would be quite a feather in my cap if I could gather you at my table and introduce you to some of my friends—"

"How many friends?" Reggie asked.

"Only a select few. People who are mad to meet all of you." Mrs. Montrose turned her attention to Miss Sanderson. "I'd enjoy having your famous employer with us."

Honey, Miss Sanderson thought, definitely is supposed to attract more flies than vinegar. She noticed that an invitation hadn't been extended to Robby's humble secretary. "I have no idea what Robby's plans are, Mrs. Montrose. Christmas is such a rushed time." She added innocently, "But I should be happy to attend one of your dinners. I've heard so much about them."

"And I would be happy to have you," the older woman told her with no outward indication of happiness. "Do try to persuade your employer to attend too." She beamed another smile at Reggie. "And you must consider it too."

He stretched long, jean-clad legs toward the fire. "I understand you have some competition now, Mrs. Montrose. A lady named—"

"Eileen Carstairs. Don't believe all you read, Reggie. I'm positive Mrs. Carstairs must have bribed the columnist to write that gushy article. He had the unmitigated gall to say that woman's dinners outshone mine. She's nothing but an upstart!"

"She *has* managed to snag some illustrious guests."

"A couple of Arab sheikhs."

"Also a Russian ballet star and two astronauts. Then there was that Spanish tenor and that chap who writes the espionage books. Quite an impressive list."

Her hand came down so heavily on the cat that it hissed and jumped down. After a moment it curled up on one of Miss Sanderson's feet. "An upstart!" Mrs. Montrose repeated. "A Johnny-come-lately!"

"You've been a hostess for many years," Miss Sanderson said.

Mrs. Montrose took a deep and apparently calming breath. "For most of my adult life. My husband, as you may know, was a career diplomat and I started to give little dinners to further his career. . . ." Her voice trailed off and she gazed moodily into space. As though speaking to herself, she continued, "I did everything in my power to further Trevor's career. He had no ambition or drive. But *I* did and I pushed and prodded until it looked as though he would receive an ambassadorship . . . perhaps even be on the honors list. Then, shortly after our son's birth . . . Trevor died. Quite suddenly. All those years of working for nothing." She gave herself a little shake and her eyes snapped back to Reggie. "I sound dreadful, don't I? But I was raised in a much different world than you. A woman didn't have the same opportunity then as one does now. In my youth women almost always had to work through a man to accomplish anything. With my husband gone my dreams were shattered. For a time I had hopes for my son, but he was exactly like his father, and so I was thrown back on my own resources. It was then I found the flair I had for dinner parties coming to my aid."

Miss Sanderson had a remarkable memory. Robert Forsythe often compared it to a computer, and now a button clicked and she remembered the reason Trevor Montrose II had lapsed into a coma. She remembered the length of time that Mrs. Montrose's child had been just marginally alive, and her heart went out to the other woman. Sybil Montrose's life had been marked by tragedy. It was her turn to pat the older woman's bony knee and say sympathetically, "You have been remarkably successful in your own right."

Mrs. Montrose said bitterly, "And now that disgusting Mrs. Carstairs is taking that away from me."

Miss Sanderson's compassion was mirrored in the dark eyes of Reggie Knight. He said slowly, "Perhaps it is time to socialize a bit. I should be honored to attend your dinner."

"And I will certainly urge Robby to be there," Miss Sanderson assured.

"You're both so kind." Simian eyes blinked and Mrs. Montrose was on her feet. "Dolly! Over here, dear. You simply must meet our latest arrivals."

In the outer room, every person with one exception was heading toward the tall young woman. The exception was the chef's wife, who had settled on the bench directly under Noel Canard's watercolor and was serenely knitting. Pale blue wool cascaded from steel needles and she didn't lift her head. The others more than made up for Alice's indifference. Felix Caspari was holding Dolly's arm, Gavin was offering her a seat, Nancy was on her other side, and Hielkje Visser was trailing behind.

Miss Sanderson had no difficulty in recognizing this celebrity. That exquisite face and figure graced dust jackets on many of her own books. Dolores Carter-White, author of dozens of outstanding romances. She looks exactly the same as she does in publicity pictures, Miss Sanderson thought, all that is lacking are the French poodles, the white furs, the white Cadillac. No, she decided, only the poodles. The white Cadillac was parked near her own car on the mainland, a white fur hung near her own jacket on a peg beside the front door.

"Felix!" Mrs. Montrose bellowed. "Don't be greedy. Bring Dolly in here. I've hardly had a chance to say hello to her."

Obediently, Felix led the vision in the white silk jumpsuit toward the alcove. The rest of the entourage followed. Mrs. Montrose hurried to meet the small parade and possessively grasped Dolly's free arm.

"Shoo!" she told the others, and tugged the younger woman into the alcove. Introductions were made, Dolly was seated beside Reggie, grog was offered by Gavin and refused, and gradually order was restored. Miss Sanderson took a long and satisfying look at her favorite author. She noticed that Mrs. Montrose, again perched at her side, was gazing transfixedly from the Black Knight to Dolores Carter-White. Miss Sanderson didn't blame her. Apart both were eye catching, but together . . .

"I didn't catch your name," Dolly said, and Miss Sanderson realized she was being addressed.

"Abigail Sanderson."

"I'm afraid . . ."

"Robert Forsythe," Mrs. Montrose told her. "His secretary."

"Oh . . . so pleased."

Mrs. Montrose was hot on the trail. "You'll be even more pleased by my news. That little dinner party I mentioned to you earlier—well, the Black Knight has accepted and Abigail will have her employer there. Now, my dear Dolly, they are just as shy as you are and—"

"I am *not* shy," Dolly said sharply. "I merely value my privacy."

"As do Reggie and Mr. Forsythe. Please reconsider."

"I'll think about it," Dolly said vaguely.

Miss Sanderson realized that the famous author spoke rather hesitantly, her voice having a tendency to trail off. Except when she had been described as shy. There had been no hesitancy then.

"Mrs. Montrose mentioned you're working on a new book," Reggie said.

Dolly replied, but Miss Sanderson wasn't listening. She was drinking the younger woman in. A creamy blonde, she observed, a tinted oval face, eyes the same shade and brilliancy as one of Robby's cherished pieces of antique green jade. The jumpsuit looked as though it had been painted onto the slender but curvaceous body. With a start she realized that Dolly looked exactly like a Christmas present she had recently purchased for a small niece. Dolly was the picture of a Barbie doll, miraculously animated and life-size. She also realized that, spellbinding as the author was, she wasn't truly beautiful. Her being seated beside Reggie Knight made that only too apparent. The Black Knight's beauty didn't stem wholly from classic features, golden skin, glossy ringlets. It was the warmth and the expression of that face that lent it true beauty.

Forcing her attention back to the conversation, Miss Sanderson found they had worked through details on Dolly's current book and were discussing the difficulties public figures encounter trying to maintain privacy. "The public," Reggie was saying, "appear to feel we're their property, that we've no right to conceal any portion of our lives from them."

"I know," Dolly assured him. "Perhaps one should expect it. After all, we're packaged goods."

Miss Sanderson bent forward. "I don't understand."

"You're fortunate," Reggie told her. "Have you seen any of the sleeves on my records?"

"I bought a couple as Christmas presents."

"And just how was the Black Knight presented?"

33

"Silk pajamas, ringlets—"

"Just where is the famous earring?" Dolly asked.

His teeth flashed whitely. "Not with me, thank God. My press agent dreamed that public image up, complete with that disgusting earring. But you're familiar with all this rot, Dolly. The furs and Cadillac."

"To say nothing of poodles," Miss Sanderson chimed in.

Dolly shifted and crossed her legs. The cat immediately leapt off Miss Sanderson's foot and lashed out, its claws barely missing Dolly's slender ankle. Hauling the animal back, Mrs. Montrose scolded, "Bad Omar! Naughty boy!" She tightened her grip on the leash. "But then, Dolly, you must be fond of pets."

"I loathe animals. Those miserable poodles are my agent's idea."

"But why?" Miss Sanderson asked.

"Like Reggie's earring. A trademark." For the first time since Dolly had entered the alcove, she smiled, tinted lips exposing perfect teeth. "And because I'm a packaged deal. Completely phony. It wasn't always that way. When my first book was published I was living quite contentedly in a primitive cottage on a delightful lonely moor. That book was published under my real name—Maud Epstein. An agent became interested and visited me there. He admired my writing but not *me*. I may not have been a beauty, but I wasn't a hag and I became huffy. I informed him all that mattered was what I put on the printed page, and Rory proceeded to fill me in on success. Any number of writers, he said, could write romances as well as I could. What I needed was a gimmick, trademarks. He said if I wanted to be a best-seller, he would handle me, but I'd have to put myself totally in his hands." She waved a hand down her long body. "And this is the result."

Miss Sanderson was fascinated. "And you went out and bought a Cadillac and furs and—"

"At that time I could barely afford food. Rory rented the clothes and car and borrowed a couple of those horrible little dogs to have the first photograph taken. It appeared on the dust jacket of my next book, and that was published under a pseudonym. Rory came up with Dolores and I made up the surname. And *voilà*! Success arrived for Dolores Carter-White." Creamy blond hair brushed over white silk as she turned her head. "I'll bet my poodles against your earring that Knight is not your real name."

"And I'd lose my earring," Reggie told her. "Day is my name. Reginald Day. I suggested Night and *my* agent stuck a *K* in front of it. Do you ever feel, Dolly, that somewhere along the way you've lost Maud Epstein?"

"Occasionally. But somewhere under all the phoniness is the real me. That I'll never lose. Will you lose Reggie Day?"

"Never! I'll always be Damien Day's kid brother."

This time Miss Sanderson didn't have to search her memory. Her face glowing, she said, "I have one of your brother's records—"

"The one and only. Damien was killed in a car crash shortly after he cut that."

Mrs. Montrose nodded her head. "I remember. He was a friend of Felix's, wasn't he? That was . . . let me see. It was years ago."

The young man's head bent and thick lashes veiled his eyes. "Nine years, three months, eleven days."

"A tragedy," Miss Sanderson murmured. "He had the most marvelous voice."

"Was he a rock singer?" Dolly asked.

"Calypso."

Mrs. Montrose pursed her lips. "If I remember correctly, he was driving Felix's car when it happened. Felix was hurt, a leg injured, I believe. Wasn't there a child involved?"

"Both a child and a young woman. Damien was killed, they were killed. Felix had a broken leg and a concussion."

Dolly placed a hand on his knee. The hand was decorative, with pearly nails and a huge opal ring that blazed in the firelight. "You must have been only a child at the time."

"Fourteen." Reggie lifted his head. "Damien was the only relative I had in this country. Our parents were dead and he was the one who got me out of that slum in Liverpool." He slanted a smile at Mrs. Montrose, but there was no humor in it. "You acted as patron for Felix, and after my brother's death, Felix acted in the same role for me. Took me in hand and arranged education and later took charge of my career."

"Felix has such a tender heart," Dolly said.

The man they had been discussing stepped into the alcove, plumped down beside Dolly, and took possession of a decorative hand. "Gavin's lighting up lamps now. Want me to have him bring one in here?"

"No," Dolly whispered. "Firelight's romantic."

"And so are you." He relinquished the hand and slid an arm around her narrow waist. She snuggled against him, making a sound much like Omar's purr. Felix nuzzled his lips against her hair.

Miss Sanderson's eyes widened and she glanced into the bar. Mrs. Caspari was still placidly knitting. Celebrities, she decided, are amazingly tolerant. Reggie, wearing a wide grin, glanced from Miss Sanderson to the chef's wife. He leaned across Dolly and told his patron, "Methinks you're shocking Abigail."

"Nothing to be shocked about." Felix's free hand caressed the opal in Dolly's ring. "We're engaged, Abigail. As soon as I'm divorced, this lovely lady and I will be married."

"*What?*" Mrs. Montrose shrieked in Miss Sanderson's ear.

"Calm down, Sybil," Felix said. "You're among the first to know."

"When? How?"

Reggie laughed. "To say nothing of where and why."

Gently, Dolly detached herself from Felix's arm. "Three months ago in Venice. We met, fell in love, Felix gave me this ring."

"But Alice?" Mrs. Montrose asked in a lower voice.

Felix shrugged a bulky shoulder. "She's dragging her feet, but she'll come around."

Still grinning, Reggie settled back. "So . . . a *ménage à trois*."

"You," Felix said hotly, "have a filthy mind. Nothing-like that. No hanky-panky. You know me. Wouldn't you say I'm a romantic?"

"With a touch of satyriasis thrown in."

Felix's thick lips twisted. "Such gratitude. You keep forgetting all I've done for you."

"No such luck. You keep reminding me."

Help, Miss Sanderson thought, I don't know if the Black Knight and the chefs' chef are going to come to blows or simply are sparring. If Robby were here, he'd have a quote from his beloved Bard that would cover this. He would also remind me of the new Abigail who has come up to date. But—she took another peek at Alice Caspari—it appears one can bring one's appearance up to date but the old mind sadly lags behind. I simply don't approve of a man bringing his wife *and* his fiancée to a party, murder or otherwise.

Apparently Mrs. Montrose, who was much older than Miss Sanderson, had no such scruples. "This is *wonderful*, my dear Dolly. Now you simply can't refuse my invitation. After all, Felix will be arranging the menu and has offered to supervise my kitchen staff. Do say you'll come."

"Don't push, Sybil," Felix told her. "Doesn't work with Dolly. Only makes her more obstinate."

Reggie said slyly, "Sounds as though you've tried pushing."

Tugging at his beard as though to rip it from his chin, the older man glowered at his protégé. Much to Miss Sanderson's relief, Fran Hornblower appeared at the far end of the bench. "Reggie and Abigail, your rooms are ready. I'll show you the way."

Reggie shook his head, but Miss Sanderson promptly rose. Felix stopped trying to destroy his beard and told her, "I'll be starting dinner shortly. Do come and watch."

She was about to make an excuse but reconsidered. It would be foolish to lose an opportunity to see Felix Caspari in action. She accepted his invitation, and as they left the alcove, Fran muttered in her ear, "You should feel honored. That's practically a royal decree."

Felix called after them, "Fran, tell Hielkje I'm expecting her to lend a hand."

"Not tonight. When she's finished laying the table I'm sending her to her room to rest. Hielkje isn't feeling well."

"Trust Gavin to have an ailing cook! Well, I'll have to make do with Alice." He bellowed, "Alice, get out to the kitchen and prepare the vegetables."

Pushing her knitting into the bag, Alice rose and scurried across the room. Fran darted an amused look at Miss Sanderson. "You're looking rather stunned."

"In some respects I'm finding it awfully hard to come up to date."

They stepped into the lobby. There was only one lamp lit there, standing on the desk beside the white queen. The chill struck and shadows danced against the walls. She headed toward the door beside the desk, but Fran touched her arm. "That's the dining room. This way." She led the way down the hall. "This is the door. Notice the flashlights on the table. At night, never go into this wing without picking up one. Gavin had pretty little niches installed in the walls of the hall for lamps and then neglected to buy extras. I tried to sneak a few out of the bars, but he made me put them back." She opened the door and shone her flash around. Doors opened from both sides of the long hall and the air seemed even frostier than it had in the foyer.

"How many rooms?" Miss Sanderson asked.

"Ten. Five on each side. But the ones on the left are unfinished as yet. The guests are all on the right. This first door"—flinging the door open, she flashed light over a rough stone wall and steps painted Chinese red—"this used to be the outside staircase on the inn. Leads up to the other two floors. When Gavin built on this wing, he had it boxed in. Claims it would make a dandy fire exit." She banged the door shut. "Anyone caught in there during a fire would be barbecued."

Miss Sanderson stepped back. The rush of air from that narrow space felt as though it originated somewhere north of Iceland. She shuddered and Fran took her arm. "You'll soon be toasty. As you'll notice, the rooms are numbered. Dolly, of course, is number one. So she can dart out of her room and get to another heated area without chilling her little tootsies—"

"You don't like Dolly?"

"I don't know her well enough to like or dislike her. Saw her for the first time this morning when I ferried out the Casparis, La Montrose, and Barbie Doll."

Miss Sanderson laughed. "Odd. That's exactly how I think of Dolly. As a gorgeous, life-size Barbie doll."

"There certainly is a resemblance. No, it's not Dolly who puts my back up. It's her fiancé. Felix issues orders as though he owns the place and perhaps he does. Anyway, room number two belongs to wife Alice, number three to

39

Reggie. Mrs. Montrose and Omar have four, and here is number five. Fitted up for that famous sleuth Robert Forsythe, and inherited by Abigail Sanderson."

"You were expecting Robby too? Nancy didn't tell you?"

"Nary a word. Gavin sent her out to snag your employer and perhaps she was afraid of his reaction when she didn't." She squeezed Miss Sanderson's arm. "I'm glad *you* came. As far as guests are concerned, with me you're *número uno*."

Miss Sanderson took a step toward her room, but Fran held her back. "Haven't finished your guided tour. Right beside your room is the lav. The bath is across the hall." A narrow beam of light settled on a door at the end of the hall. "The outside door opening onto a cold, windy night. Now, into your room."

"Blimey! I can see where a large chunk of Gavin's money went."

The room was spacious, the furnishings appeared to be antique, a fire blazed on the hearth, a lamp sat on the dressing table, another beamed yellowish light from beside the canopied bed. Miss Sanderson touched the mellow surface of a Queen Anne dressing table. "Are these reproductions?"

"Genuine. Even the lamps. Observe the hand-painted globes. Some items were already in the inn, and Gavin rummaged antique shops for the rest. He'd planned to furnish all ten guest rooms but could barely get five done. Scrimped on the construction of this wing to do that." Fran thumped a paneled wall. "Behind this pretty walnut is not enough insulation to stop a summer breeze."

"Didn't Nancy intercede?"

"Nancy has no say in the Jester. That's Gavin's baby. And Felix aided and abetted him. Until he realized there

40

weren't enough funds left to cover the creature comforts he dotes on. Then Felix raised hell."

"Is Felix a partner?"

"No idea, but he must have put up some money. Gavin seems broke, and Nancy had only a little insurance from her mother's estate. And I rather doubt Gavin could have raised loans to cover what he's done here. Anyway, Felix was back and forth all the time this place was being tarted up, getting in the way and giving orders. Hielkje and I learned to detest the man." Grinning, Fran added, "Hielkje calls Felix a *sjoelke* and it fits."

"What is a *sjoelke*?"

"Frisian word meaning a spoiler. A person who grabs for himself. And Felix certainly grabbed the VIP suite for himself." Fran glanced around the room. "Couple of scuttles of coal over there, and I tucked a bottle of brandy and some glasses in that chest. Towels and so on in this drawer. Anything else you need?"

"Not a thing. Oh, where's my case?"

"In the wardrobe. I unpacked for you. That's a gorgeous chiffon dress, but better keep it for London. The fireplace in the dining room doesn't draw properly and I had to move in a kerosene heater. It's better than nothing, but the room is still on the chill side." Fran glanced at her watch. "I'd better herd Hielkje up to her room for a rest."

"She looks ill."

"She is. By the way, I'm driving her in to see her doctor tomorrow afternoon. Like to come along? Finchley's a pretty little place."

"Yes, I'd like that. And, Fran, thank you."

"Nothing but the best service at the Jester. Oh, better have this." She handed the flash to the older woman. "I noticed you brought one with you, but an extra could come in handy. I'll grope my way up the hall. I'll see you later."

Watching the brown ponytail jauntily bobbing away,

Miss Sanderson thought: That's one person who is also *número uno* with me. Quick moving, competent, overworked, and still finding time to be kind. Peggy Canard had been fortunate and so was Nancy. But it was a mystery why a woman with Fran's obvious ability would choose to close herself away in this desolate spot. She shrugged. None of her business. Wandering around the room, she felt content. Even if she hadn't been exactly a welcome addition to the party, she was glad she had come. She paused in front of the fireplace and glanced up at the gilded frame over the mantel. Another of Noel Canard's watercolors, and she regarded it warily. After a time she relaxed. Nothing in this one that jarred. He had exercised the same charm in this scene that he had used with his little skaters. A tawny-haired little girl, dressed in a blue dress and pinafore, was gathering daisies in a field. She was stooping, a few flowers clasped in one hand, the other reaching down into the grass for another. Sunlight glinted on her round face, and her hair looked as though a breeze was stirring it. Then Miss Sanderson stiffened. Nearly hidden in the grass, its color and markings acting as camouflage, was a coiled snake. One eye glistened and it was reaching toward the dimpled hand. She sensed its bite would be poisonous.

Shaking her head, she looked for and found a towel and her sponge bag. As she opened the door, she felt curiously reluctant to step into the cold darkness of the hall.

CHAPTER FOUR

CLOSING THE DOOR OF THE BEDROOM WING BEHIND HER, Miss Sanderson placed the flash Fran had given her on the hall table. There were about a dozen lined up and they were an odd lot, large and small, new and old, cheap and expensive. Not unlike the guest wing. The bathroom sparkled with Dutch tile and extravagant fixtures, and the water flowing from the hot water tap was tepid.

Turning down the hall toward the rear of the inn, Miss Sanderson adjusted her black woolen skirt and pulled down the white angora sweater. She had taken Fran's advice and left her new gown on its hanger. Lucky she had brought this outfit. It wasn't spectacular, but it was warm. She pushed on a green baize door and found a stonefloored kitchen and Felix Caspari, resplendent in crisp white jacket and towering chef's hat, working at a long, scoured table.

"Abigail," he called jovially. "Take a chair and watch this cook at work."

Miss Sanderson took a chair near the other spectator. Dolly Carter-White, lavish in a floor-length gown and the fur cape, was perched on a high stool. The gown was split to the thigh and revealed a slender, shapely leg. The hand bearing the opal ring toyed with a pendant. Emerald, Miss

43

Sanderson thought enviously, one perfect stone dropping from a platinum chain. The emerald was close to the color of the writer's eyes.

The third member of what Reggie had called the *ménage à trois* was darting around the kitchen, from the stove to the sink to the table where her husband presided. Alice had also changed, but she looked as dowdy in the long brown gown as she had earlier. If Dolly resembled a bird of paradise, Alice looked remarkably like a sparrow.

Felix said genially, "I'm hampered by these deplorable surroundings, but I did bring my own knives. Fortunately, I never travel without them." He waved at a pigskin case resting at one end of the table. Miss Sanderson peered at it, and the chef obligingly tilted the case. Nestled on green felt was an array of knives. The smallest was only about two inches long, and the largest looked as though it could hack its way through the toughest jungle. Selecting one, he held it up. "This is the most useful and my favorite. Six-inch blade of finest steel set into an ebony handle. It's a matching set and was made up especially for me. Now, I begin."

The knife blade flashed and he began. Miss Sanderson noticed another flash from the handle. She whispered to Dolly and was told that all the knives had Felix's initials in gold set into the ebony. As she watched, she marveled at the man's speed and dexterity. He didn't make a false move and seemed able to use both hands and his tongue at the same time. He lectured about the dishes being prepared, complained about the Jester's kitchen, and gave orders to and scolded his wife. It seemed Alice could do nothing right. Miss Sanderson marveled at the woman's forbearance. If it were I, she thought grimly, that chef would be wearing one of his sauces.

Time passed and Miss Sanderson had no comprehension of how much. Not only was it fascinating to watch, but the odors of food were making her mouth water. Lunch seemed a long time in the past, and her stomach was groaning audibly. Finally, Felix carefully wiped his favorite knife, whipped off the towering hat, and spread his arms wide. "A feast worthy of royalty," he said modestly. Taking off the jacket, he threw it to his wife and held out a gallant hand to Dolly.

Miss Sanderson rose. "Can I help with the serving?"

"Of course not. Alice will handle it, and by this time that dratted Hielkje should be rested enough to help. Come along."

The dining room was as chill as predicted. The rest of the party members were waiting, and Hielkje was dispatched to assist in serving. Several small tables had been pushed together to provide one long enough for the ten diners. Felix sat at the head of the improvised table with Dolly on his right, Nancy Lebonhom on his left. Miss Sanderson selected a chair between Reggie and Fran and blinked when she saw the Jacqueline-of-all-trades. The ponytail had been brushed into long sheaves of shining brown hair, the jeans and pea jacket replaced by a knitted dress and matching jacket, her long face was touched with makeup. Fran Hornblower, she decided, was not only a fine woman but a fine-looking one.

Fran turned her gleaming head. "How did you enjoy your introduction to Felix's art?"

"He knows his business."

"That no one can deny."

"His knife set wouldn't look out of place in a jewel case."

"And probably cost as much as diamonds and pearls."

Reggie moved restlessly. "I'm starving."

"Rescue is at hand," Miss Sanderson told him as Hielkje trundled in the first course.

Miss Sanderson never forgot the menu for that meal. As

45

she later told Forsythe, each course was not only superb but also couldn't seem to be topped until the next arrived. Chestnut soup was followed by ambrosia salad, salmon mousse with a lobster sauce, and then lemon sorbet to clear their palates. With those palates fresh and tingling they were regaled with stuffed trout and a dish modestly named *Viande de Boeuf* Caspari. The roast duck had a dressing that contained walnuts, apricots, and currants, and the sweet was a fluffy confection that smelled of brandy and tasted like heaven.

With dessert Hielkje and Alice took their places and started to catch up on their own dinners. Felix made no effort to be polite to the kitchen staff. He dusted off his mustache, threw down his napkin, and rose. Helping Dolly from her chair, he announced. "Hielkje will serve coffee in the saloon bar. This room is like a refrigerator."

Fran's eyes shot sparks. "Not by Hielkje and not in the saloon bar. She's going to have her dinner, and I didn't get around to lighting a fire in there. You'll have to use the public bar."

"Alice," Felix snapped, "you handle the coffee."

Miss Sanderson had had enough. "I'll do it," she said, and stalked from the room. To her surprise, when she reached the baize doors she found that Alice Caspari was close behind her. "You should finish your dinner," Miss Sanderson scolded.

"I'm not hungry. Handling all that food rather destroys an appetite. This won't take long. Everything is laid out. You fill the creamer and sugar bowl and I'll put the coffee on." Alice measured coffee and confided, "This is the only job that Felix trusts me with except for preparing vegetables and that sort of thing." She lifted faded blue eyes to the older woman. "What did you think of dinner?"

"Any meal from now on is going to be an anticlimax."

"He's wonderful, isn't he?" Alice pinkened with pleasure. "An artist!"

Miss Sanderson resisted an impulse to kick the woman. It was obvious that Alice, despite her husband's treatment, adored the brute. Takes all types, she thought. For every tyrant there's a victim. Aloud she asked, "How long have you been married?"

"Nearly twenty years. But we've been together for much longer." Alice lifted the coffeepot onto a metal serving wagon and wheeled it toward a door Miss Sanderson hadn't previously noticed. "This way's shorter, Abigail. Through the saloon bar. Oh, I forgot. There won't be lamps lit in there. We'll have to go down the hall. Would you get the door, please."

Miss Sanderson held open the baize door and the wheels of the wagon clattered over red and black tile. Impulsively, she asked, "Aren't you . . . don't you . . ." She couldn't find the words. How do you ask a devoted wife whether she resents her husband's fiancée?

"You're thinking of Dolly Carter-White," Alice guessed, and then giggled. "You can't expect Felix to act like other men. He's had dozens of love affairs, but they never last long. Women just can't resist him."

This woman can resist him, Miss Sanderson thought. "But he intends to *marry* Dolly."

"That's just because he can't get into bed with her any other way," his wife said bluntly. They had reached the doors leading to the public bar, and Alice waited while Miss Sanderson opened one. As she pushed the wagon in, she whispered, "But first he must divorce me, mustn't he?"

The entire household was gathered in the bar. Gavin, looking rather self-conscious, was posted behind the bar, toying with a pile of cardboard folders. Mrs. Montrose, the gray cat perched on her lap, was seated at one of the tables, chatting with Reggie Knight. Near them Fran was talking

47

to Hielkje. Miss Sanderson noticed that Hielkje's thick brown hair, earlier worn in a bun, had now been arranged in elaborate coronet braids. Nancy was perched on a barstool, and Felix and his fiancée were cuddling on a bench in the alcove. Their heads were close together and Felix seemed to be nibbling at a tinted cheek. His wife, assisted by Miss Sanderson, handed around coffee.

Balancing two cups, Miss Sanderson joined Nancy Lebonhom. She handed the girl one, climbed on a high stool, and glanced down the bar at Gavin and his folders. The one on the top was labeled "Confidential," and under it, in capital letters, was typed DOLORES CARTER-WHITE. Ah, the scripts for the murder game. Alice Caspari returned from taking coffee to her husband and Dolly and, instead of filling a cup for herself, approached the counter. She whispered to Gavin and he turned and peered up at the rows of bottles. Alice pointed and he took down a bottle of jenever, selected a tulip-shaped glass, and handed them to Alice. The next time Miss Sanderson noticed the woman she was in her favorite spot, on the bench under the watercolor, knitting and drinking schnapps.

Miss Sanderson turned to Nancy. "Have your husband and Felix been friends for long?"

"Only since Gavin and I were married. I was the one who introduced them. You must remember—" Nancy gave a rueful little laugh. "I keep forgetting, Auntie Abby, you know little about me. Well, at one time I had aspirations for an acting career, with about as much luck as Gavin has had at writing. But I did get a job on a TV show as an assistant to Felix—"

"The cooking show?"

"Yes. Did you see any of them?"

"Unfortunately, no. You say you were his assistant?"

Honey-colored curls shook. "That was my title, but what I actually did was hand the great chef utensils, stand

48

around looking decorative, and 'oohed' and 'aahed' when he gave me tastes of his creations. Felix called me his official taster." Nancy nudged the older woman. "Looks as though Gavin is ready to give his spiel."

"This seems most important to him."

Nancy laughed again. "He's been practicing his speech in front of a mirror."

Clearing his throat, the writer called, "Attention, everyone."

The hum of conversation faltered and then ceased and heads turned toward the counter. Shooting a look of annoyance toward the alcove, Gavin raised his voice. "Dolly, Felix! Would you please join us?"

They stepped out of the alcove, but Felix looked bored and slightly resentful. "Couldn't this wait for a while?"

"No. After all, this is the reason for this party. I know the others are eager to hear what I have to say."

None of the others seemed overeager to hear his words. Mrs. Montrose appeared more interested in petting her cat than in Gavin, Reggie wasn't trying to hide the fact he was as bored as Felix, and Fran was yawning. Alice continued to knit, but the bottle and glass had disappeared. Miss Sanderson blinked. The only place those two objects could have gone was into the capacious knitting bag.

Clearing his throat again, their host fumbled with the folders. "Now, kindly attend. Any questions you wish to ask will be answered after I explain the . . . hem, the ground rules. To simplify this game I have used your own names as the names of the characters you will portray. Of course, that will be the only resemblance. I have a folder here for each of you, and in each is a comprehensive history of your character's background. There is also a script, showing the dialogue you will be required to give. The dialogue is important because it will display to our charming detective"—his mustache quivered as he beamed a smile in Miss Sanderson's direction—"certain clues. You must also memorize the details on your background because you must play fair and answer Abigail's questions honestly—"

"What did you cast me as?" Felix asked.

"Not as a chef, but you will enjoy your role. One point I stress is that under no circumstances are you to allow any of the others to see your material. In effect this might—"

"Do the murderer and the victim know that he or she *is* the murderer or victim?" Reggie asked.

"Of course." Gavin smiled slyly. "But that might be *victims*. That is the reason the folders must be protected from other people. Knowledge of either of these points would ruin the game. Now, as I call your name would you step up and—"

"Names," Mrs. Montrose said. "I feel you should have given us fictitious ones. It would be more interesting."

"As I said, dear lady, this will simplify things. And your own names are most interesting. As an example, take my name. I've never met anyone else having the same surname."

"It is unusual," Mrs. Montrose agreed.

"I believe it comes from Norman times. I have often fancied an ancestor might have been the Sieur le Bon Homme." Gavin proceeded to enlarge on his theory. "And you, Mrs. Montrose, must also be a descendant of a Norman conqueror."

"My husband was and better he than me. A pink mountain!"

Fran laughed. "I hate to blow my own horn, but my ancestor must have been the great Hornblower. Reggie, you may be a descendant of Sir Lancelot—"

"If you can picture that knight with a heavy tan," Reggie told her. He turned to Hielkje. "We know Abigail's the son of a sander. What about you?"

"Visser. A fisherman."

Fran seemed to be enjoying herself. "Caspari I can't do anything with, although it does sound a bit like a laxative, but Dolly . . . Ah, a cart and white horse."

"Or a carter with a white dog," Reggie chimed in.

Gavin pounded the counter with his fist. "Come to order! This is getting a bit ridiculous."

"No more so than considering you're a good man," Felix said.

Gavin pounded harder. "I call this meeting to order! Allow me to finish and then we'll have a nightcap." Gradually the meeting came to order and Gavin continued, "The only person without a script is Abigail. She will have to listen, observe, question, and attempt to outwit the author. And I must warn you, Abigail, that won't be simple. This script is a masterpiece of misdirection—"

"I hope," she interrupted, "you aren't going to spring facts on the last page I haven't had access to."

"Certainly not. I've played fair, but there are numerous red herrings."

"She'll solve it." Nancy put an arm around Miss Sanderson's thin shoulders. "Auntie Abby can smell out a fish at ten paces."

"We'll see." Her husband fingered his mustache. "Any or all of the rest of you may attempt to solve the case. If none of you do—"

"The great author will be willing to expound," Felix said caustically.

"True. Your expertise is in a kitchen, mine is behind a typewriter. Any questions?"

Reggie stretched his slender frame. "When is the game afoot?"

"I'd hoped to begin tomorrow." Gavin darted a sour look at Hielkje. "But Hielkje must be taken in to Finchley, so we'll start at lunch the day after tomorrow and—"

51

"Come now," Felix protested. "My time is limited."

"And so is mine," Reggie said.

This was one item Gavin obviously hadn't practiced in front of his mirror. He flushed, gulped, looked at his wife, and when she shrugged, said placatingly, "The game won't take that long. Abigail will have twenty-four hours to come up with a solution, and if she fails, I'll take over and then you all can—"

"Twenty-four *hours*," Miss Sanderson wailed.

"Boo!" Fran called. "Dirty pool."

"Robert Forsythe could have done it," Gavin said smugly.

A challenge, Miss Sanderson thought, and she picked up the gauntlet. "You're on."

"Now, folders and that nightcap." Gavin held one up. "Dolly."

In a swirl of silk skirts, white fox, and a heady perfume, the folder was gracefully accepted. "And a touch of cognac?" Gavin asked.

Felix's arm crept around his fiancée's waist. "My cognac and in my suite."

Reggie looked interested and ambled over. "I know the quality of that cognac, Felix, and I'm tagging along for a drink."

Gavin handed out folders and asked, "I thought you never drank anything but beer?"

"I said seldom, not never." Taking his folder, Reggie held out a gallant arm to Dolly.

As she took that arm, Felix scowled, and then his face relaxed. "Fine. Like me to carry your folders for you?"

"Dolly, Reggie." Gavin leaned over the counter. "Watch Felix and those folders. He's crafty."

Dolly waved hers. "Word of honor on a cart with a white horse he won't see mine."

"Nor mine." Reggie made a graceful and sweeping bow.

"To take a peek at this he'll have to joust with Sir Lancelot."

As the three headed out of the bar, Miss Sanderson declined a drink and crossed the room to refill her cup. She noticed that Alice Caspari and her knitting bag had vanished. When she returned to her stool, the rest of the folders had been dispensed. She asked Nancy, "It's Felix that Gavin is concerned about with the scripts, isn't it?"

"None other, and Gavin has reason to be suspicious. Felix has a nasty sense of humor."

Gavin, carrying a brimming glass, joined them. "Felix is a confirmed practical joker. Nan, tell Abigail about that deal he pulled on the French chef."

His wife's hazel eyes glinted wickedly. "It happened on the TV show I was mentioning. A noted Parisian chef named Lebois was Felix's guest, and sly old Felix switched the paprika and the cayenne. The joke was supposed to be at my expense as I was usually the one who tasted and cried, 'Superb!' But this time Lebois raised a spoonful of a sauce laden with cayenne, told the studio audience and thousands of viewers, 'Zis will tempt taste buds,' and gulped it. He promptly spewed the stuff right across the counter at the camera."

Miss Sanderson howled with laughter, but Gavin wasn't laughing. He said grimly. "Tell her about the camera crew."

"This one was far from funny. The lads from the camera crew loved Felix's dishes, and after the show he let them devour the food he'd prepared. One day he made éclairs, which they were mad about, and the topping he concocted was that strong chocolate laxative. The poor devils bolted the éclairs, and some of them were off work for a couple of days. One of the older chaps was quite ill."

"Not funny," Miss Sanderson agreed.

"This one *was*." Gavin, now wreathed in smiles, leaned across the counter. "Nan says that after the Lebois debacle

Felix tried to shift the blame to her by telling the irate chef it was her fault the bottles had been switched."

Giggling, Nancy took up the tale. "But Lebois had heard all about Felix's practical jokes and he wasn't fooled. He got a beautiful revenge. Lebois conspired with one of the camera lads and they dusted Felix's white jacket and chef's hat with itching powder. On the next show..." Hopping off the stool, Nancy pantomimed scratching at her head, digging into armpits, jumping and grimacing and squirming.

This time Miss Sanderson laughed until tears started to her eyes. "I should have watched that show," she gasped. "It *was* live?"

"Very much so. In fact, that was the liveliest show of the series. The viewers loved it."

"You can see," Gavin said earnestly, "why we can't allow Felix to see those other scripts. He'd figure out something devilish that would make me a laughingstock. I've worked hard and I'm damned if I'll let him ruin it, even if he is—" Breaking off, he called, "What's up now, Fran?"

"There's still the mess from dinner to clean up."

"Isn't Hielkje doing it?"

"She started to, but she was dropping in the traces so I bundled her off to bed."

Gavin swore and turned on his wife. "That ruddy woman! I told you we should have replaced her."

"But Hielkje was so kind to Mother."

"Kind or not, we simply can't keep on this way. If she can't handle the work, she'll have to go."

Pushing a strand of hair behind an ear, Fran told him, "Gavin, she has no place to go."

"I'm not running a nursing home."

"After we get some medication for her tomorrow she'll

54

be feeling better. Right now I'm looking for kitchen volunteers."

"Don't bother looking at me." Mrs. Montrose rose and picked up her cat. Over her shoulder she called, "And I don't do floors either."

Gavin glared at Fran. "You can be so embarrassing! Now you've offended Mrs. Montrose."

"Tough," she said, and looked hopefully at Nancy.

The girl sighed and climbed off her stool. So did Miss Sanderson. "I'll help," the secretary told her.

Gavin made no objection to this and sat, watching the three women gathering up cups and piling them on the serving wagon. Fran called, "Gavin, I'll expect you on fuel detail in the morning."

"You'll be disappointed. I've scads of work to do."

"You remember the bargain we struck? I told you we had to put on extra staff for this party and you said—"

"That we couldn't afford it."

"So we compromised. Nancy's to help Hielkje, you are to help me. Nancy's keeping her part of the bargain, but you haven't lifted a finger."

"All right!" He flung his hands up. "Don't nag. I'll help bring in the filthy coal."

Fran turned to her assistant. "Abigail, you finish up here and bring this stuff along to the kitchen. Don't forget the ashtrays. Nancy, we'll start washing up."

Miss Sanderson asked, "Shall I bring the dishes from the dining room?"

"Hielkje managed to gather them up." With Nancy in tow Fran briskly headed toward the lobby. Over her shoulder she called, "Gavin, no later than nine or your celebrities are going to be freezing."

He glared after her and told Miss Sanderson, "A regular Simon Legree."

"You're fortunate to have her."

"I suppose so. Fran does all her own work and half of Hielkje's. Funny, she can do anything. Not only runs the boat but fixes it up if anything breaks down. She can repair plumbing and does carpentry better than most of the high-paid carpenters we had in to build on the guest wing."

"I wonder where she picked it all up?"

Gavin poured himself another generous drink. "Somewhere in the Middle East. One of those bleeding heart liberals who went to refugee camps in Palestine and so on. A ruddy waste of time. Taking care of a bunch of terrorists!"

Miss Sanderson had piled the top of the wagon high. She bent to stack ashtrays on the lower shelf. "There are women and children there too. Hungry and sick. Perhaps if there were more people like Fran Hornblower, there would be fewer terrorists."

"Sounds as though you're another bleeding heart."

Shrugging, she changed the subject. "Nancy looks exhausted."

"She doesn't sleep well." Moodily, he gazed into his glass. "I had the devil's own time getting her to agree to keep this place on. Complains it's too isolated, but I know what's really wrong. Nan's frightened out of her wits of her father's ghost. Thinks—"

"Ghost?" She straightened and stared at him. "Noel Canard?"

"Ever heard such rubbish? When we came to live here, there was still an old couple in that fishing village on the mainland. A Sam something and his wife. They were moving into Finchley, but before they left they managed to fill Nancy full of their wild tales. Claimed a number of times they'd seen a black-clad figure crossing the causeway. They told her that's why they were leaving. Noel Canard, in his mask, was coming to get them."

For once Miss Sanderson agreed with Gavin. "Surely Nancy doesn't believe that superstitious nonsense?"

"She lets on she doesn't. But several times I've roused in the night and she's sitting straight up in bed, listening, white as a sheet. Always claims she's heard a sound." He tossed back the rest of his brandy. "Naturally she hears sounds in an old building such as this one. Creaks of timbers and that sort of thing. I keep trying to jolly her out of it. This morning I told Dolly and Felix about the old fisherman's ghost story and both of them were amused. Nancy was there and I was glad to see her smile." He thumped his glass on the wagon and stretched. "Well, I'm off now. If I'm going to lug coal in the morning, I'd better get some work done at my desk before I turn in."

They parted in the hall, Gavin heading up the staircase, Miss Sanderson wheeling the wagon down the hall. Only the single lamp in the foyer behind her was lit, and the hall was so dark she was tempted to snatch up a flashlight from the table. She was glad to reach the baize doors and nudge them open. The kitchen was warm and bright with three lamps lit. Fran was up to her elbows in steaming, sudsy water, and Nancy was drying dishes. "Bring the cart over here," Fran told her. "Then you can start sticking china in that cupboard. The cutlery goes in those two drawers. Hielkje and Alice must have washed up between courses, so we shouldn't be much longer."

Nancy hung a damp dishcloth and reached for a dry one. "If Gavin hadn't been so stubborn, we'd have electricity and could chuck all this in a dishwashing machine."

"And if pigs had wings they'd be soaring like gulls," Fran told her. "Cheer up, Nancy, it might be worse. Anyway, a couple of days and we'll be back to normal."

"And how long will it be before my dear husband decides to throw another murder party?"

"He'd better hold off until he can put modern conveniences in. The wealthy clientele he's hoping to attract will never stand for this. Atmosphere or no atmosphere."

57

They worked at top speed and finally Fran pulled the plug in the sink and reached for a sponge. "I'll finish mopping up here. You two trot along. Thanks for the help. If I discover any floors to be done, I'll bypass Mrs. Montrose and get you two. Abigail, remember to pick up a flash. You too, Nancy. I wasn't able to get that lamp at the top of the stairs lit and it's going to be blacker than hell up there." She called a cheerful good-night, and Miss Sanderson and Nancy groped their way along the hall.

Nancy was clutching the older woman's arm, and Miss Sanderson squeezed the girl's hand warmly to her side. "I told your husband, Nancy, that you're lucky people. With Fran, I mean."

"Don't I know that! Mother was lucky too. At first she had no intention of taking either Hielkje or Fran on. Hielkje wasn't well, even then, and Mother didn't think Fran could handle the heavy work around here. Mother was looking for a couple, the woman for housework, the man for the boat and the other chores. But she liked both of them and took a chance. As Mother told me, Fran is worth two men and she's a wonderful nurse too. Mother couldn't have had better care than Fran gave her." They reached the table and groped for flashlights. Miss Sanderson found hers was long and heavy with a worn rubber grip.

At the foot of the stairs, she turned to say good-night. Nancy still firmly clasped her arm. "I was wondering, Auntie Abby, if you'd like to come up to my sitting room. When I was sorting through Mother's boxes, I found some school pictures you might like to see. I recognized you in them immediately."

"It's been a long day. Perhaps tomorrow?" Nancy bobbed her head but retained her hold. Switching on her flash, Miss Sanderson beamed it up the staircase. She wondered if the girl was nervous about going up there alone. "Heck," she said. "No time like the present. Lead on."

They started up the stairs. Nancy switched her own flash on and shone it ahead of them. "Mother—" The girl broke off. As Miss Sanderson glanced at her, Nancy's mouth opened and she gave a piercing shriek. Her body went limp and she sagged heavily against the older woman.

Miss Sanderson beamed her flash upward. Standing at the top, motionless, was a tall figure in dark clothes. It was wearing a black mask.

CHAPTER FIVE

THE FIGURE MOVED, AN ARM LIFTED, IN ONE HAND something glinted. A knife? Taking her cue from Nancy, Miss Sanderson screamed.

"For God's sake!" the figure said. "Have you never seen a ski mask before?" He ripped off the mask and glossy ringlets tumbled to his shoulders.

Miss Sanderson hardly had enough strength to lower the girl to a step. Releasing the older woman's arm, Nancy wrapped both arms around her legs. "*Father*," she whimpered.

"The Black Knight," Miss Sanderson told her.

Their screams had been heard. Thrusting Reggie aside, Gavin raced down to his wife. A creamy blond head bobbed over the singer's shoulder. Gavin ordered, "Someone get that damn lamp lit up there." He bent over his wife's crumpled body. "What in hell is wrong with you, Nan? Did you fall?"

Miss Sanderson tried to detach the clinging arms, but Nancy held on to her legs like a limpet to a rock. "She's had a scare," the secretary told Gavin, and added shakily, "And so did I."

Felix Caspari had joined the group above them and the

lamp was now showering a splash of yellow light over the landing. She could see that what she had thought a knife was actually Reggie's silver flask.

Gavin, now understanding the reason for his wife's collapse, cut loose at Reggie. "You damn fool! What in hell do you think—"

"Will someone explain what this is all about?" Reggie asked plaintively. "As soon as I know, I'll offer an apology."

"Forget it," Gavin rasped. He tugged at his wife. "Come on, Nan, I'll get you up to bed."

"I'll help," Miss Sanderson said. "Nancy, let go of my legs—there's a good girl."

Between them they got the girl up the rest of the stairs, down the hall, and into a small and cosy sitting room. Here there were not only lamps glowing, but a fire beamed warmth. Gavin lifted his wife to the sofa and Miss Sanderson scooped up an afghan and spread it over her. Pushing back his untidy hair, Gavin said, "I'd better get you brandy."

"No." Nancy's face was still colorless, but she managed a weak smile. "I'll be fine. Sorry to act like an ass, darling, but it was so dark and when I flashed the light up . . . You go along, Gavin. Auntie Abby, would you . . . ."

"Of course." Miss Sanderson told Gavin, "I'll stay with her for a while."

"Well . . . all right, but she should be in bed." He paused by the door. "If you need me, I'll be in my study. And, Abigail, try and talk some sense into her. She's becoming a ruddy neurotic."

As the door closed the girl began to weep. Sinking down beside her, Miss Sanderson found her handkerchief and handed it over. "Gavin's right," Nancy sobbed. "I am becoming neurotic."

"That makes two of us. I panicked as badly as you did."

"It's this place. Not a neighbor for miles. Just rock and water and wind. I don't know how Mother ever stood it here." She mopped at wet eyes. "I'm used to cities and swarms of people and traffic and noise."

"I think there's more to it than that."

"Has Gavin . . . Yes, I can tell he has."

"He told me about the old fisherman's ghost story."

"And you think I'm *mad*." Nancy clutched her curly head in both hands and rocked back and forth. "Gavin thinks so too, and sometimes I agree."

"I do *not* think you're mad. Let's talk this out. Let's—" Miss Sanderson stopped abruptly. She had been about to suggest they lay ghosts to rest. Hardly tactful. "Surely, you're not frightened of your own father?"

"I never really knew him—"

"You must have memories. You said you were fifteen at the time of his accident."

"When I was a child, I didn't see that much of either Father or Mother. He was stationed in so many different places, and Mother always tagged along with him. She was devoted to him, and when it came to a choice between Nancy and Noel, it was no contest. Until I was old enough for boarding school, I was farmed out between a grandmother and a great-aunt. After Father was so badly disfigured, I never saw him again. All I knew was that he'd turned into a recluse and always wore that damn mask."

It would have been kinder, Miss Sanderson thought hotly, if the girl had been allowed to see her father's ravaged face than have to imagine what lay behind that mask. Aloud, she said gently, "You know there are no ghosts."

"Do you?"

"Yes." The older woman was glad that at that moment Robby wasn't with them. He was the one who always teased her about being fey. He was also the one who had tried to persuade her that there had been no ghost haunting

62

the studio of Sebastian Calvert. She repeated firmly, "Yes."

"What if it isn't a ghost?"

"What are you trying to say?"

"His body was never found. He was a strong swimmer." Nancy was twisting the handkerchief as though trying to wring her tears from it. "What if he isn't *dead*?"

Despite the warmth of the cosy room, Miss Sanderson felt chill fingers running up and down her spine. There was more than a ghost to lay to rest here. This was nightmare land. She pulled herself together. Use logic, she decided. "What would be Noel's purpose in feigning death?"

"I'm certain he was . . . his mind was gone. After that horrible fire on his ship he was never normal. Does a madman have to have a purpose?"

"Even madness must, Nancy. Perhaps later in his life Noel was not normal, but I once knew him. Granted it was many years ago, but people don't change that much. Noel was very handsome and quite narcissistic about his looks. It must have been a terrible blow to him when his face was badly burned. But the man I knew was far too fond of comfort and ease to have voluntarily left the source of it."

"Mother?" Nancy nibbled thoughtfully on her lower lip. "That does make sense, Auntie Abby, but you must look at his paintings in order to understand how deranged he'd become. They're ghastly things. I keep telling Gavin that, but he refuses to see the horror in them. Gavin tells me it's my imagination." She continued to punish the handkerchief.

"It's not your imagination. I've seen it too."

"A man capable of that is capable of anything."

The girl's chin had set stubbornly, and Miss Sanderson resisted an impulse to shake her. Continue with logic. "Tell me this. How is a man with a mask covering a badly scarred face going to find shelter, food, fuel, around here?"

"I'd never thought of that! Father had no friends left,

not one person to help him. . . ." Flinging her arms around Miss Sanderson's neck, she hugged her. "I've been a fool! Father *is* dead and his ghost does *not* walk. Poor old Sam and Maggie were simply wallowing in superstition. Thank God you came down here!" Nancy glanced at the mantel clock and said contritely, "You must be exhausted. Look at the time."

Miss Sanderson was only too aware of the time. It was nearly two. She stood up and straightened her skirt. "I'm off to bed and you'd better head for yours. Want me to wait until you're settled?"

"Not necessary." Pushing aside the afghan, Nancy hopped up. "Gavin will soon be in, and I promise I'm not going to be a ninny anymore. That's over."

"Your husband will be glad to hear it. Gavin's been worried about you."

Picking up the heavy flashlight, Miss Sanderson opened the door. Nancy rushed to kiss her. She looked up at the older woman. "All Gavin is worried about is keeping me from selling this place. Good-night, Auntie Abby, and thanks."

For a moment Miss Sanderson stood outside Nancy's room. Nancy and her writer husband had been married for less than a year. Judging by the bitterness in the girl's voice, it looked as though their honeymoon was definitely over.

Across from her a door banged open and light spilled across the floor. Felix Caspari, an arm anchored as usual around his true love's waist, said, "Still up, Abigail? I'm walking Dolly back to her room. That performance you and Nancy put on shook her up."

If Dolly was shaken, she certainly didn't show it. Not a hair was out of place and the oval face was serene. Biting back a sharp retort, Miss Sanderson asked, "Where did Reggie get the ski mask from?"

"I gave it to him." Felix murmured. "Careful on these stairs, Dolly. That lamp doesn't shed much light."

At the bottom of the staircase the lamp didn't help at all, and Miss Sanderson pressed the button on her flash. "You brought a ski mask with you?"

"Hardly. I found that one when I was rummaging around in the attic. Reggie's always complaining about Jamaicans feeling the cold, so I gave it to him." He added, "He also helped himself generously to my brandy. Even filled his flask."

Miss Sanderson held open the door to the guest wing. "Better take a flash," she told the younger woman.

Dolly shrugged. "I don't really need one. My room's only a few steps down the hall."

When Felix opened the door to room number one, light spilled out and the air from the room seemed delightfully warm. It was also delightfully scented. Miss Sanderson peered past Dolly's shoulder. On an ornate dressing table flamed a huge bouquet of crimson roses. It would seem Dolly was number one in more ways than one. Felix and Dolly were now ignoring her. They were locked in a passionate embrace. She glanced from the lovers to the roses, smiled, and started down the hall. At that moment the door of room number two was flung open. Mrs. Caspari lurched into view. She managed to lurch into the doorframe, and the sharp juniper odor of jenever mingled with the fragrance of hothouse roses.

Alice was draped in a billowing nightgown and she had loosened her hair, holding it back from her face with a velvet band. Lamplight was kind to her, and Miss Sanderson realized that as a girl this woman must have been extremely pretty. Ignoring the secretary, Alice said, "So, Snow White and the seventh dwarf. Dopey!"

"I believe the one with the beard was Doc." Having

65

corrected her rival, Dolly detached her lissome form from the chef's arms.

"Looks and brains both, eh?" Alice hiccuped and swayed. "Listen up, Snow White. You want to sleep with Dopey, feel free. He's slept with dozens of other sluts. But forget about trotting up the aisle in a veil. I am *Mrs. Caspari*, and I'm damn well going to stay Mrs.—"

"Alice!" Mr. Caspari roared. "You've had your bloody nose in jenever again. Why in hell—"

"Wasn't talking to *you*," Alice roared back. "Talking to Snow—"

"Shut your mouth, you bitch! Get back in that room or—"

"Or what, Dopey?"

Felix, his handsome face twisted with rage, took a step forward and raised his fist. "Want another taste of this?"

"I really wouldn't, Felix," a voice said. Reggie Knight was belting a robe around his slender waist.

The older man's arm fell and he muttered, "Well, *you* shut her up then. You know how she gets when she drinks."

Reggie moved up beside Miss Sanderson. "Never interfere in family fights. Not unless they get violent. Get it off your chest, Alice."

Alice tried to focus her eyes on her husband. "Not giving you a divorce. Not now or never. Paid a price for you, and I earned the right to stay your wife. You're *mine*."

For an instant it looked as though, Reggie or no Reggie, Alice was going to get her husband's fist in her face. Then Felix gave a deep sigh and gently pushed Dolly into her room. He closed the door and the lamplight was cut off. From the shadows his voice came and it was deathly quiet: "I belong to no one, Alice. Certainly not to you. Dolly and I will be married and you won't stop us. If necessary, I'll fake evidence against you."

Alice's voice was softer too. "You know all about that, don't you?"

There was no answer. A door creaked and Miss Sanderson decided that Felix had slipped back into the inn. Alice stood in the light shining from her room, tears pouring down her cheeks. Reggie stepped to her side. "Show time's over, Alice. To bed and sleep it off." As gently as Felix had handled his fiancée, Reggie handled Alice. Closing the door, he turned to Miss Sanderson. "Nasty, wasn't it?"

"I think I'm in shock. I never saw a mouse turn into a raging lion before."

"Only happens when Alice gets her nose in the schnapps. And she rarely does that. Never accomplishes anything either. Felix is something of a lion tamer."

"Using his fists?"

"On occasion. Not when I'm around."

He opened his bedroom door. "Care for a nightcap? I just happen to have some vintage brandy."

"So I heard. Purloined from the chef's private stock. Not tonight, Reggie. Like Hielkje, I'm stumbling in the traces."

"Is Nancy all right?"

"I hope so. That was a dumb thing to do."

"Still haven't the foggiest what I *did* do." He stretched. "I'll be off too. Been a long day."

Too long a day, Miss Sanderson thought, as she glanced in the mirror over the dressing table. Her silver curls were rumpled and her face looked as old as Mrs. Montrose's. She made record time in climbing under the down duvet. The sheets were icy, and she settled shivering into a little ball. Before she was warmed through she was asleep.

She roused once, heard what sounded like stealthy footsteps in the hall, and then settled back. That, she told herself firmly, is an example of the many sounds buildings make. Expansion or contraction. Definitely not Noel Canard, alive or dead, with a hideous face behind a black mask, coming to get me.

And then, drowsily, she remembered a plume of smoke funneling from a chimney in the deserted village across from the Jester.

CHAPTER SIX

Morning arrived with light filtering between the curtains, a metallic clanking in the hall, a soft tap on the door. Starting up in bed, Miss Sanderson peered at her traveling clock. Only a few minutes after eight. The night had been as short as the previous day had been long. She thrust back the duvet and reached for her robe. Blimey, but this room was cold. She padded across the carpet and swung open the door. Fran, wearing jeans and her pea jacket, was bending over a serving wagon. Her hair was stuffed up under a navy watch cap. "Morning," she said cheerfully. "Sleep well?"

"Like a log. Breakfast?"

"Continental style. Which means coffee and a roll. Easier than setting up a table. You seem to be my only taker."

Miss Sanderson glanced down the hall. "Mrs. Montrose was the only one with sense enough to get to bed at a decent time."

"Bunch of nighthawks." Fran poured coffee from an insulated jug. "If they figure they'll make up at lunchtime, they're going to be disappointed. Hielkje is just going to stick something on the buffet. Better take more rolls, Abigail. Bran muffins this side, poppy seed the other. Ah, another customer. Morning, Reggie. How goes the knight-errant business?"

"Booming. What's in the pots?"

"Honey, marmalade, and raspberry jam. Better follow Abigail's example and load up. As I was just telling her, lunch will be light, and unless Felix handles dinner, it may come out of tins. Abigail and I are taking Hielkje to Finchley this afternoon. Care to come along?"

"Think I'll hang around the Jester. It may be cold, but we have great floor shows here." Taking a plate, he heaped it.

Fran pushed the creamer closer. "I heard about the show on the stairs. Seems you did a star turn. Gavin has cooled off now, but it's obvious he wanted to deck you last night. Why on earth did you pull a ratty trick like that?"

Miss Sanderson picked up her plate and mug. "Fran, Reggie knows nothing about the ghost of the Jester."

"But Reggie is going to find out and right now," the Black Knight said.

"Not from me." Fran set down the coffee jug. "I have to rout Gavin out for fuel detail, and that's going to be almost harder than doing the job by myself."

With a clatter of wheels against tile, she bounced down the hall. Miss Sanderson was turning toward her room when Reggie stopped her. "Come into my boudoir and tell all. I'm dying to hear about the Jester's ghost." He added coaxingly, "I've a nice fire going and I'll bet you haven't."

The fire was blazing and cast a circle of warmth around the hearth. Reggie put his breakfast down on a hassock and brought over a side table for Miss Sanderson's. Thinking of her own room, unmade bed, clothing thrown over chairs, she was amazed at the neatness of his. The bed had been made and everything was tidy. On a fine Regency chest his silver flask perched beside a ship's clock. He reached for the flask and poured a dollop into her coffee mug. "You look as if you could use a pick-me-up. Now, tell all."

She told him about Nancy's fears, and his dark eyes blazed. "That bloody Felix! Conned me again. His lousy jokes!"

"That one was a sick sort of joke." She took a gulp of coffee and lifted a muffin dabbed with honey. "How did he manage to get you to put on the ski mask?"

"He kidded about my Jamaican blood, brought out the mask, and said I should wear it to go down to the guest wing. Keep me from turning to ice in the halls." Reggie spread butter and marmalade and flung down the knife. "I'd had several tots of his booze and it sounded like a good idea. But this is a bit rough even for Felix. Maybe he didn't know about Nancy's—"

"Gavin told Dolly and him about it yesterday. Did he suggest you look up Nancy?"

"No. But he did say I should show the galley slaves in the kitchen the Black Knight's new look. And he probably suspected Nancy would be there. Abigail, I feel terrible. Poor Nancy. Seeing that figure looming over her on the dark staircase. God! She might have had a heart attack."

"She didn't," Miss Sanderson pointed out. "And perhaps in a way, it wasn't all that bad. We had a talk. I'm hoping I might have lanced that abscess of hers." She finished her last bite and settled back, flipping open her cigarette case. They sat in companionable silence, the only sound the hissing of coal on the grate. After a time she murmured, "Might better get it off your chest."

"How do you know I want to ask a favor?"

"All I know is that you're working yourself up to something. And I hardly think you get up early every morning to tidy your room. You were waiting for me."

He glanced at the neatly made bed and his teeth glinted. "Remind me never to try and conceal anything from Abigail Sanderson, girl detective. Very well, cards on the table. I want you to use your influence with your boss. Ask him, persuade him, I hope, to look into something for me."

Blowing a smoke ring, she regarded it. "That's one card. Turn over a few more."

"Can't you take me on faith? I know Forsythe will be intrigued. Tell you what, I'll autograph those record sleeves you bought for Christmas presents."

"This is connected with your brother's death, isn't it?"

"Perhaps the detective I need is sitting opposite me. Expound, Holmes."

"Watson. Bumbling along. Also elementary." On long fingers she ticked off points. "Your reaction to not meeting Robby—out of proportion. Mrs. Montrose's I could understand. She was hoping to snag off an illustrious and rather elusive celebrity. That remark you made about being interested in old cases. The look on your face when you spoke about your brother's death. More anger than grief."

"Remind me never to play poker with you." He pantomimed spreading cards on the hassock. "Damien and Felix went to a party at a country home. One of the swinging ones with lots of sex and booze and drugs. When they left in the wee hours, they got into Felix's car, a new Jaguar, and according to a maid, Felix was behind the wheel. His story was that before they pulled out of the driveway, he realized he'd had too much to drink, so Damien and he changed places. Felix also claimed that Damien had been drinking heavily and had been snorting nose candy—"

"Cocaine?"

"Yes. Felix said he dozed off in the passenger seat, and when he came to, the car was careening off the road and the next thing he knew an ambulance attendant was bending over him." Reggie's hands balled into fists. "Two people had been walking along that road. A young woman and a three-year-old kid. They'd been on their way home, their car had run out of petrol, and they were walking the rest of the way. According to the police, Damien crashed into them, killed them, lost control of the Jaguar, and smashed it against a tree. No witnesses and Damien was dead. They had to take Felix's word for the details." He looked directly into Miss Sanderson's eyes. "I *know* Felix was driving that car."

I'm too soft, she thought. I feel like patting his head and sympathizing. Just like Watson. Now, make like Holmes. She threw her cigarette butt into the grate and said evenly, "Your reasoning?"

It was his turn to lift a pink-palmed hand and tick off fingers. "Point number one—Felix's nature. No way he'd ever let anyone else drive his new car. Two—if Damien had been drinking and doping, why let him take the wheel? Three—Damien seldom had more than a glass of wine or a pint of beer. And he *never* took drugs—"

"You're certain? You said you were only fourteen at that time."

"When I was younger than that, I learned how my big brother felt about drugs. I was about nine and we were still living in a tenement in Liverpool. A gang of kids were in the alley behind the rattrap we lived in. One of them had come up with a couple of joints—"

"Marijuana?"

"Yes. We were passing them around, feeling like big men, when Damien came up behind us. The other kids took one look at him and took to their heels. Damien caught me and held me off the ground with my face on a level with his." Reggie rubbed an upper arm as though his brother had just released his grip. "Lord, but he was strong! He didn't raise his voice, told me in this level deadly tone that if I wanted to ruin my life, commit suicide, he'd finish me right there. Said he'd bash my head in. And he meant it." Reggie reached for his mug, found it empty, and put it back on the hassock. "Our parents had gone down the drain with alcohol. Both of them opened and closed the pubs. I loathed them, but Damien could remember when they first came here, and he kept telling me they should never have left Jamaica, that they simply couldn't adjust. He said they'd lost to alcohol, but we weren't going to lose to anything. Damien took me away from Liverpool and found a job in London. He was working as a dishwasher in a restaurant when Felix Caspari heard him singing in the kitchen. Felix took him up and it looked as though Damien was going to make the big time, but . . ."

But he had died before he had, Miss Sanderson thought. "You said Felix paid for your education—"

"I said arranged. When Damien started to work, the first thing he did was to take out an insurance policy on his life. He had a tough time making the premiums, but he said if anything happened to him, I'd be looked after. Felix took care of me in an impersonal sort of way, but once in a while he'd do something kind and rather touching for me. Funny, people have so many sides. Most of the time Felix is a selfish, egotistical monster, but occasionally he makes impulsive, generous gestures."

"And you want Robby to look into the accident, try to find proof that Felix was driving the car that night."

"Exactly. You see, Damien Day isn't remembered because he was a worthy human being with a tremendous talent. If he's remembered at all, it's as a drug-soaked swinger who ran down and killed a woman and a child. I want his name cleared. For once I want Felix to take his own medicine."

"That won't bring your brother back, Reggie."

"I know that only too well. But it's important to me."

She was tapping a thumbnail against a front tooth. Reggie cocked his head. "What's that in aid of?"

"A bad habit, and one Robby complains about. It helps me think."

"And what are you thinking?"

She took another cigarette. "I've a feeling you're holding something back."

He slid to his knees and started to build up the fire. The ringlets fell forward, veiling his face. "I was saving this for Forsythe, but I'd better tell you. About six months after Damien's death I was visiting Felix and Alice for a few days. Felix's injuries had healed and he was back to normal. Had a hot new love affair going, and as usual, Alice was pretending to be ignorant of it. She bottles it up and then goes on a schnapps binge and all the venom comes spewing out—"

"Like last night."

"Similar. But this time Alice waited until Felix was out of the house, and then she called me down to his study. She handed me a letter she'd found while she was ransacking his desk." He poked at the grate and a lump of coal rolled across the hearth. "There was a check for a generous amount in it that Felix had had his solicitor send to the husband and father of the dead woman and the child. The man had returned it. He said he wouldn't accept blood money from his family's killer. He said he'd talked to the police constable who'd arrived first at the accident site, and the constable was sure that the driver of the Jaguar hadn't been Damien Day. He was a rural cop and rode a bike. The Jaguar had passed him moments before the accident, and although the visibility was poor, he'd had the impression the driver had a beard."

Miss Sanderson jerked forward. "Why didn't the police pursue this?"

Reggie looked bleakly up at her. "Put yourself in their place. When the car crashed, both Damien and Felix were thrown into the rear of it. They were jumbled up together, impossible to prove who had been behind the wheel. No witnesses, and Felix swore that Damien had been driving. The only evidence, the word of a lowly constable who admitted he'd only had a glimpse and the visibility was poor. But as far as I'm concerned, I agree with the man who wrote the letter and returned Felix's check. Conscience money!" He picked up the tongs and threw the lump of coal on the grate. "Will you speak to Forsythe?"

"I will, but I must warn you there's slight chance even Robby can prove your brother's innocence. About the only thing that can do that is a confession from Felix Caspari."

Reggie smashed the tongs down. "I'd like to choke it out of the bastard!"

"Easy." She rose, adjusted her robe, and patted his shoulder. "Violence won't help. Let's wait and hear what Robby says."

She left him, still kneeling, looking gloomily into the flames. He looks as though he's praying, she thought.

CHAPTER SEVEN

M ISS SANDERSON BARELY HAD TIME TO DRESS AND neaten her room before Gavin Lebonhom, without bothering to knock, came puffing in. He lugged two scuttles that pulled his shoulders down. His hair spilled over his brow, he had a black smudge on his nose, his expression resembled a thundercloud. His response to Miss Sanderson's greeting was a grunt.

"Shake a leg," Fran bayed from the hall.

Muttering a curse, Gavin grabbed up the empty scuttles and banged out of the room. Fran stuck her head into the room. "Lunch is laid on in the dining room, Abigail. Better have a bite. Happy boy and I will soon be finished, and after I wash up, we'll head for Finchley."

"Your assistant seems far from happy."

"It's good for him. Gavin's far too sedentary."

The buffet lunch turned out to be a savory beef stew and crusty bread. The long table had been dismantled, and the small tables had been returned to their places. Miss Sanderson dished up stew and made her way to the table where Mrs. Montrose and Nancy were seated. Nancy looked as fresh as a flower. The young, Miss Sanderson thought enviously, how resilient they are. Nancy has the nerve storm and I'm the one who shows its effects. Omar left his mistress's side and put a fluffy paw on Miss Sanderson's knee. She dipped a crust into the bowl and proffered it. He sniffed, gave her a disdainful look, and stalked back to Mrs. Montrose. "Omar," that lady stated, "is terribly fussy about food. Quite spoiled."

Glancing around, Miss Sanderson noticed that only Gavin, Fran, and Mrs. Caspari were missing. She knew what Gavin and Fran were doing. Alice . . . probably nursing a giant-size hangover. Her husband appeared to be in an expansive mood and was regaling Dolly and Hielkje with what, judging from their laughter, had to be a hilarious story. In a corner, Reggie, seated alone, was paying more attention to them than to his meal. As Miss Sanderson finished her stew, Fran came bouncing into the dining room. She'd taken off her watch cap, brushed her hair into a glossy ponytail, but was still wearing jeans and the pea jacket.

"Hielkje, Abigail," she called. "Captain Hornblower is ready to set sail."

Hielkje and Miss Sanderson headed toward the lobby. The cook bundled up in a moth-eaten fur coat and a heavy headscarf, and as they stepped out of the inn, Miss Sanderson heartily wished she had a fur coat, moth-eaten or otherwise. Although the sky was clear and watery sunlight fell across their faces, the wind was even colder than it had been the previous day. As the speedboat cut through the choppy water, she looked searchingly at the deserted fishing village. No smoke funneled from the stone cottages.

The women made their way toward the cars, and Miss Sanderson asked, "Is the Mini yours?"

"Gavin's," Fran told her.

The little car was covered with dust and a fender was deeply dented. "Shall we take my car?" Miss Sanderson asked.

Fran dug into a pocket, extracted a ring of keys, threw them up, and caught them. "We ride in high style." She headed toward the Rolls, unlocked doors, flung a rear one wide. "In you go, Hielkje, and pull that rug over your lap. Abigail, you sit in front and help me navigate. Never driven one of these things before."

Fran handled the big car as she did most things, with quiet dexterity and ease. Miss Sanderson ran an admiring hand over the walnut dash. "Did you, by any chance, pick Felix's pocket?"

"Perish the thought! He pressed the keys in my hot little hand and told me we'd be more comfortable using this beauty. Odd chap. Drives one mad most of the time and then does something surprisingly kind. Felix also told me not to worry, he'd cook an informal dinner tonight."

That streak of impulsive generosity Reggie had mentioned, Miss Sanderson thought. Leaning forward, Hielkje touched Fran's shoulder. "What mood is Gavin in today?"

"Beastly. He was just recovering from the indignity of fuel patrol, and then he came storming out of his study and cornered me in the hall. Positively livid with rage. Accused me of opening a window and scattering papers all over his desk. I tried to tell him there was no way *I* would open his damn window. Not after working like a fool to keep the place warm, but he kept on ranting. Finally I shouted back. Asked how I could get into his ruddy study to do anything when he keeps it locked like a vault."

"And then he calmed down," Hielkje said.

"Wrong. He yelled something about Nancy having left the connecting door to their bedroom unlocked and went tearing off to give her hell."

Miss Sanderson opened her cigarette case and offered it to her companions. When they shook their heads, she lit one and observed, "Gavin is far from a model employer."

"You're seeing him at a bad time," Hielkje said. "Right

79

now he's so tense and nervous. Trying so hard to make his party a success."

Glancing over her shoulder, Miss Sanderson noticed that Hielkje looked nervous and tense. Worried about her health or job? Probably both. She sighed and settled back to enjoy the comfort of the car, the scene unreeling outside her window. Not that the view was inspirational. Sunlight didn't make the desolate downs any more attractive. Today she didn't even spot any sheep grazing, and it was a relief to turn onto a more traveled road. Here at least were signs of life. A petrol station and some cottages broke the monotony, and an Alsation rushed from a drive to challenge the Rolls. Fran swung the car smoothly around a tractor trailer and pointed a finger. "There's Finchley, Abigail. Market town and not large, but seems a metropolis after the Jester. Now, battle plan. We'll drop Hielkje at the clinic and then—"

"Fran, it may take quite a while. Dr. Parker wants to make tests."

"Not to worry. I have to buy supplies and do some errands. You stay put in his office and I'll pick you up there. Abigail, what would you like to do?"

"Look around the shops. I still have a couple of presents to get."

"With all the party panic, I keep forgetting how close Christmas is getting. Oh, well, my list is short."

"So is mine," Hielkje said dolefully.

"Count yourselves fortunate," Miss Sanderson said. "I've scads of nieces and nephews, to say nothing of brothers, sisters, and in-laws."

Fran smiled rather sadly. "You're the fortunate one, Abigail. Now, where to meet. How about the local pub?"

"Rather a busman's holiday."

"At least they won't force you to help wash up. There's a tea shop that does a lovely cream tea."

"Sounds more like it."

The Rolls drew up in front of a square, ugly building and Fran hopped out and opened the door for her friend. Miss Sanderson noticed she hugged Hielkje before the stout woman started trudging up the walk. An elderly man with an elderly mongrel on a leash paused to admire the Rolls, and a boy with a Mohawk cut slowed his moped to make a rude gesture. Miss Sanderson promptly made it back and his eyes widened.

Fran slid back behind the wheel. "Think the locals had never seen a Rolls before." She caressed the walnut wheel. "Wish I owned this honey."

"And if pigs had wings—"

"They'd soar like gulls." Fran chuckled. "I'll drop you off here. Tea shop a block farther down. Don't spend all your money."

Miss Sanderson had no intention of being extravagant. Her new look had been too costly. A small gift for Mrs. Sutter, she decided, a slightly larger one for Robby. She glanced around the heart of the town. It didn't look as though progress had spread its ugly plastic and chrome and garish colors far in Finchley. The inn didn't look much younger than the Jester, and she was tempted to step inside and see if it had the same charm. You'll have enough atmosphere before you leave the island, she thought, and strolled on.

A window display caught her eyes and she stopped. There were twin pyramids of books, one a historical romance, the other a cookbook. She grinned. On the back of one dust jacket a dazzling Dolores Carter White leaned against a Cadillac, hugging a white poodle to a fur-covered bosom. Felix Caspari, handsome in jacket and chef's hat, beamed from the front of the other. The future bride and groom. At least if Felix could bully his wife into divorce, they would be. She was about to move on and then changed her mind. The perfect gifts for Mrs. Sutter, who doted on romance and history and cooking. Not only that, but for no extra cost the books would be autographed by their authors.

She loved bookstores, but she resisted the impulse to browse and was soon back in the street clutching a package. The moped breezed by and she stared at the rider, wondering whether they were about to enter the lists again. This time the boy turned his shorn head away and ignored her. Never let silver hair fool you, she told him silently. I give as good as I get.

Now for Robby. Ah, an antique shop with a tasteful display of chamber pots in the bowed window. Something small and not too expensive. Perhaps a smoking stand or bookends. A bell tinkled over the door, and at the desk a woman wearing a severe black dress and rhinestoned glasses raised a sleek head. She waved an expansive hand. "Do wander around. If you need assistance, give a call."

Miss Sanderson wandered around. She picked up a brass elephant, shook her head, replaced it, looked covetously at a fine Spode fruit bowl, and passed on. She examined a pipe rack made of bamboo and shook her head again. Then she spotted a case of jade ornaments. Keep away from that, she warned herself, though Robby loves jade and has quite a nice collection. No champagne tastes on a beer budget. Then she found herself leaning over the glass top, staring down at the piece in the dead center of the velvet lining. She tried to lift the top, but it was locked. Magically, the clerk appeared at her elbow, turned a key in the lock, and lifted the glass. "Which one are you interested in, madame?"

Miss Sanderson pointed, and the jade was placed tenderly in her palm. It was exquisite. Each limb of the tree, each green leaf was perfect. Pink flowers blossomed, and near the top a minuscule white jade bird threw back its throat in silent song. Silent? For an instant Miss Sanderson thought she could hear that song. Rhinestoned Glasses was now murmuring something about Han dynasty, and Miss Sanderson opened her mouth to tell the clerk to replace it in the case. To her horror, she asked the price, which was revealed in a mere whisper. Just as well not to shout *that* amount. Miss Sanderson saw Robby's face as he opened a Christmas parcel, peeled back tissue, glimpsed this beautiful thing.

"Will you take a check?" the disembodied voice that was her own was asking.

Not only was a check acceptable, but arrangements were made to send the jade tree to Miss Sanderson's London flat. When she reached the cold, windy street this time, she was deep in shock. Abigail Sanderson, she lectured herself, you're insane. Your bank account is depleted and you'll suffer the indignity of having to borrow from your ancient cook. And Aggie might be old, but she was canny and charged excessive rates of interest on her loans.

Anyway, that finished not only her bank account but her shopping. She trotted along and located the tea shop. By the time that Fran joined her, she was seated in a corner munching a Bath bun and sipping strong hot brew. Ordering the cream tea, Fran peered at her companion's plate. "Rather a frugal tea."

"Economizing. Good thing Christmas comes only once a year."

"I told you to watch your spending. But be of good heart. You'll be able to feast on Felix's cooking when we get back to the Jester." The younger woman shoved back her sleeve. "Lots of time. Those tests are drawn out. I hope Hielkje is bearing up."

"You're awfully good to her. Have you been friends for long?"

"We met when we were both interviewed by Peggy

Canard. Less than two years ago. Answered the same ad. Hielkje was overawed that Peggy's daughter was the girl she saw on her favorite cooking show. But neither of us had much hope that Peggy would hire us. She wanted a married couple and didn't believe I could handle the maintenance work. When she found I had nursing experience, she decided to take both of us on trial. We made out fine and Peggy was quite pleased with us."

"At that time Peggy wasn't well."

"A heart condition. I could see that at a glance. All the signs. Bluish lips, shortness of breath. She lived only eight months, but we made her as comfortable as we could. Nancy came down to the island a couple of times and seemed relieved her mother was well enough looked after that she wouldn't have to concern herself. Nancy and Peggy weren't close." Fran cut into a cream-covered scone. "I had my hands full. Hielkje was ailing too. Finally Peggy and I forced her to go to Dr. Parker for treatment. Her problem was what I'd thought it was—thyroid. There was no reason for her to be ill, and medication put it right in no time. But Hielkje had neglected to take care of it herself. She has rotten luck. Last summer she had hepatitis and was terribly ill. She'd only started to pull out of that when she began to show her present symptoms." Fran sighed. "Practically a walking case history."

"You sound more like a doctor than a nurse."

"I'm not even a nurse. At least I haven't a degree to prove it. Picked nursing up the way I've picked everything up—by trial and error. I've even assisted with operations. Once David and I removed an appendix by the light of a couple of flashes."

"In the East?"

"Someone's been gossiping about my past."

"Gavin mentioned you once worked in refugee camps."

"And called me a bleeding heart. He was wrong. Those

camps harden hearts. It's necessary or you'd bleed to death."

"And you worked with doctors?"

"One." Fran stirred milk into her tea. "David was an idealist . . . no, that's the wrong term. His was a practical dedication. Amazing man. Didn't care about race, religion, creed. All the world was his family."

"He's not heavy," Miss Sanderson said softly, "he's my brother." Fran nodded and Miss Sanderson asked, "Was?"

"He's dead. Killed in Beirut. There was a car bombing—"

"He was killed by a bomb?"

"David was shot. Gunned down by a policeman with an itchy trigger finger. David was running to help a child wounded by the bomb." Fran looked up. There were no tears in her brown eyes, only insufferable grief. "When he was killed I went berserk. Flung myself at the policeman and told him to shoot me too. Kill everyone! Kill the people who have come to nurse your sick, save your children!" Fran's voice had risen, and at the next table two plump women turned to stare. One, Miss Sanderson noted, had a smear of cream on a puffy chin. She stared coldly back and the women lowered their heads over their plates. "Sorry," Fran whispered. "David and I . . . we were lovers."

"So you came home and buried yourself on that godforsaken island."

"I have no home. I came back to England determined to give up the senseless crusade. Let them suffer and die. My heart bleeds no more."

Wrong, Miss Sanderson thought, your heart bleeds for David, who is dead, for Hielkje, who is alive, and must have for Peggy Canard. One cannot turn compassion such as that off like a tap.

Setting down her cup, Fran buttoned her pea jacket to the throat. "We'd better see if Hielkje is ready, Abigail."

The Frisian hadn't waited in the warmth of the doctor's office. She was standing on the walk in front of the clinic, huddled in the ratty fur coat. As Fran bundled her into the car, she scolded, "Hielkje Visser, you have the makings of a martyr and try my patience something fierce."

"It looks serious, Fran."

Sliding in beside Miss Sanderson, Fran stared through the windshield. "How serious?"

"Dr. Parker didn't say. He has to wait for the results of the tests, but . . . what if he has to operate?" Hielkje started to cry. "What am I to do?"

"The obvious. If an operation is needed, you're going to have it. Did he give you medication?"

"Some pills. He said they'd help. Fran, Gavin will fire me!"

Fran switched on the ignition and the car purred away. "No, he won't. You'll have the operation and convalesce and your job will be waiting."

"But how? Nancy?"

"Nancy is right under his thumb. She can't do anything. But I can. If you go, I go. Think it's going to be easy to replace us? Most people would prefer the dole to living in that place. And how would Gavin enjoy using his delicate hands for manual toil?" Fran snorted. "He can't even get the ruddy boat started."

Hielkje blew her nose and wiped at her wet face. She managed a weak smile. "You're so good to me."

Miss Sanderson slanted a smile at Fran Hornblower. "The crusade goes on."

Fran said rather bitterly, "Old habits are hard to break."

CHAPTER EIGHT

THAT EVENING FELIX SERVED HIS DINNER IN THE SALOON bar. He had Gavin light a fire, and a number of brass lamps, shaped like ship's lanterns, cast a yellowish glow over the dishes spread the length of a refectory table. The saloon bar was smaller and more comfortable than the public bar. There were a number of side tables, and the faded brocade chairs were deeply cushioned. As Miss Sanderson joined the line to fill her plate, she reflected that the only informal part of dinner was its setting.

Alice Caspari wandered in and silently took a plate. The lion of the previous night had vanished and she was again a timid and subdued mouse. Taking a heaped plate, Miss Sanderson chose a chair near the fireplace and tucked in. As she dribbled lingonberry preserve over crisp Camembert fritters, she found she was regarding Felix more kindly. Whether it was the scrumptious food or the ride in his Rolls, she couldn't quite decide. He was also entertaining, amusing them with tales of his career.

After a time, Hielkje put in an appearance and carried her dinner over to the chair beside the secretary's. "Fran's battening down the hatches," she told the older woman.

"It's working up to a storm and at this time of year they can be wicked."

Nancy joined them and perched on a footstool. "This is my first winter here and I'm not looking forward to it. It's bad enough in the spring and summer."

"Stop complaining," her husband told her tartly. He softened his tone. "There's nothing nicer than curling up in front of a roaring fire with a good book on a winter's night."

"Provided there's enough coal to keep that fire roaring." Fran Hornblower pushed past Gavin and stood on the hearth rug, rubbing her hands together. Her cheeks were glowing with color. "Foul night and it's going to get worse. By the way, Gavin, fuel duty at seven tomorrow morning if you want to start your drama on schedule."

Gavin took the order almost cheerfully. Smiling, he looked around. "Has everyone memorized their lines?"

"I haven't," Mrs. Montrose said flatly. She fed a bit of veal to her cat. "I've enough on my mind without doing that. I'll have to read from my script."

Hielkje colored faintly and glanced guiltily up at her employer but said nothing. Fran, who was bending over the buffet table, called, "I'll have to read too."

Gavin scowled and Felix clapped a hand on his shoulder. "Cheer up, old man. I've committed my role to memory and I'm certain Dolly has too. Writers have marvelous memories."

"We have to have," Dolly admitted. "But this time I don't have to use mine. I've no lines and—"

"*Dolly*," Gavin blurted.

"Sorry, Gavin, completely forgot my vow of silence."

And so much for Barbie Doll's marvelous memory, Miss Sanderson thought. Also, her first clue. She was mulling this over when Dolly rose, stretched her lithe body, and deposited a kiss on her fiancé's cheek. He hugged her close. "What's that for?"

"A thank-you for the wonderful dinner and a good-night."

"Surely you're not going to bed so early."

Playfully she tugged at his short beard. "I'm going to put in a couple of hours on my book and then get some much needed beauty sleep."

Felix rose promptly to the bait and declaimed on the futility of beauty sleep for such a gorgeous creature. Smothering a yawn, Dolly slipped away from his grasp and called a general good-night.

As the door closed behind Dolly, Nancy heaved a deep sigh and pulled herself off the footstool. "Hielkje, I suppose we better start the washing up."

Felix stopped being romantic. "Alice will have to help you, Hielkje. Nancy, I want to talk to Gavin and you."

Pouting, Nancy put a hand on Miss Sanderson's shoulder. "I was hoping to have some time with Auntie Abby. We haven't had a chance for a decent chat."

"Sorry, but pleasure must give way to business."

"Business?" Gavin frowned. He brushed at his waterfall mustache. "What's this all about?"

"It may be a bitter pill, but"—Felix laughed—"you can wash it down with some of my excellent brandy. We'll have our board meeting in my suite."

Gavin looked apprehensive and his wife was still pouting, but they followed the chef into the foyer. Sticking her knitting back in the bag, Alice started to clear the table and pile the dishes on one of the serving wagons. Hielkje rolled in another wagon and helped her. Mrs. Montrose, her cat curled peacefully up by her feet, bent her fluffy gray head over a book. For once Fran didn't whip around working. She sank into the chair vacated by Hielkje and draped her long legs over the footstool. She chatted with Miss Sanderson, and then the older woman glanced at her watch and rose. "I'd better get to bed before I fall asleep right here."

"Reggie already has," Fran said.

The Black Knight was sprawled on the sofa, his arms folded over his chest. Miss Sanderson said good-night to Fran and Mrs. Montrose, patted the cat's head, and then paused by the sofa. In sleep Reggie looked so young, she thought, so innocent and so beautiful. His older brother, she recalled, hadn't possessed much claim to good looks. Damien had been taller and heavier than Reggie, and his skin had been darker, a blue-black. But his voice . . . ah, that had been as smooth and golden as his brother's skin was.

She trotted down the hall and picked up a flashlight. She opened the door to the guest wing and found the flash wasn't immediately needed. Strong light fell through the doorway of room number one. As Miss Sanderson stepped into the light, Dolly appeared in the doorway. She was draped in something diaphanous, and the lamps behind her silhouetted her figure and gilded the ends of her hair. Her face was in shadow. She jumped and gasped, "Who is it?"

"Abigail. Did I startle you?"

"A bit. This place is so . . . so spooky. Well, I'm off to the bath and then bed."

"I'll walk down with you." Miss Sanderson snapped on her flash and pointed the beam on the floor. Dolly thudded into Miss Sanderson's shoulder. "Sorry," she said, then asked brightly, "All ready to start detecting?"

"Ready as I'll ever be. Hey, that's not the bath. That's one of the unfinished rooms."

"So it is. Yes, here we are."

"You'd better take the flash."

"You'll need it."

"I have one I brought with me in my room."

"Ta-ta and good-night."

Reaching past Dolly, Miss Sanderson opened the door of the bath. A lamp, the wick turned down low, sat on the tile sink, casting a dim light. Dolly walked in and managed to thud her shoulder again, this time on the doorjamb. Miss Sanderson stood in the dark hall wondering what was wrong with the woman. Could Dolly, like her rival, have had her nose in a bottle? There had been no smell of alcohol around her, but she'd acted tipsy. Drugs?

Miss Sanderson shrugged and groped her way across the hall toward her own room. She came up hard against a door and found she was entering the lav. Trailing a hand along the wall, she located her doorknob by banging a hip against it. A fine person to mentally accuse Dolly of being in her cups. Here she was, sober as a judge, ricocheting off doors and walls. Well, I can certainly do something about being sober, she decided, heading toward the chest where Fran Hornblower had secreted the brandy.

As she sipped, she noticed that Fran's prophecy about the storm had come true. The shutters on her window were banging and clattering.

Miss Sanderson not only slept soundly that night but managed to sleep in the next morning. She had just finished tidying her room and was pulling a heavy cardigan over a rolled-neck sweater when a knock sounded at her door. It was Reggie, dressed as warmly as she was and wearing a wide smile. "Twelve o'clock high," he told her. "Force-ten storm raging and lunch is being served in that deep freeze they call a dining room. The game will soon be afoot. How is Holmes today?"

"More like Watson than ever."

"Try positive thinking. Think yourself into Holmes's clever shoes. Tell you what, I'll act as your Dr. Watson."

"For all I know you may be the murderer I'm trying to root out."

He waved his folder. "Aha, for me to know, for you to wonder."

As they wandered down the hall, she asked, "How is our host this morning?"

"Like a cat on a hot stove. Acts like the weight of the world rests on his shoulders. Gavin has opening-night jitters."

They passed the desk and she pointed at the glass queens. "Whimsical touch."

"They don't seem to fit the Jester. Clowns would be more suitable." He opened the door of the dining room and told her, "The orders are to take separate tables. Supposed to be a group of strangers."

With the exceptions of the host and hostess, who were seated at the table nearest the door, the guests were occupying their own tables. The tables were covered with snowy linen and each was ornamented by a crystal bud vase displaying one artificial carnation. The room was merely chilly, not frigid as it had been when Miss Sanderson had last dined there. She spotted the reason. Another heater had been moved in at the far end of the room. Hopefully she checked out the table beside it and found she was out of luck. Mrs. Montrose and Omar had snaggled that one, and Reggie had quickly taken the cosy table near the other heater.

Miss Sanderson pulled out a chair and plumped down at the table behind his. Behind her the wind and rain clawed icily at a windowpane. As Reggie pulled his chair closer to the heater, she shivered and muttered, "The days of chivalry have vanished. Knight-errant, indeed!"

"Blame it on my Jamaican blood. Either too thick or too thin for this climate. Never can figure out which—Hey! Look at Fran. Talk about figures. And legs. A shame she covers that shape up in denim most of the time."

Both of the Jester's employees were carrying sandwich

trays and cheese and fruit plates. They were dressed as French maids from a drawing room comedy, complete with short black dresses, lacy aprons, and black net hose. Their hair was upswept and topped with jaunty lace caps. They wore flimsy black sandals with four-inch heels. The outfit suited Fran and displayed the trim figure and splendid legs that Reggie was admiring. Hielkje was less fortunate. With her stout torso and thick legs she looked like a sausage stuffed into a decorative casing. But she was handling the high heels more expertly than Fran was.

Teetering over, Fran proffered a sandwich tray. Reggie leered up at her and whispered, "*Où là là*. And when do you get off work, *ma petite*?"

"Soon," She winked at him. "Wait outside the kitchen door for me. That should cool you off, *mon garçon*."

Selecting a sandwich, Miss Sanderson asked, "When do we begin?"

"Anytime now." Fran held up her script. "But I haven't much to say. I think Gavin must have given Hielkje all the good lines."

As Fran moved unsteadily away, Miss Sanderson glanced around. The other guests seemed engrossed in their luncheons and their scripts. Gavin had a thick folder at his elbow, but he was bending over the table in what looked like a heated conversation with his wife. Reggie nudged Miss Sanderson. "Notice that two of the cast are missing?"

Mrs. Montrose was trying to interest her haughty Persian in a scrap of sandwich, and Alice Caspari was casting on stitches, this time using a dreadful shade of purple wool. "Ah, no sign of the lovebirds."

"Amazing, Holmes. I've no idea how you do it."

"Keep this up and you can do the detecting and I'll play your part."

At that moment Gavin Lebonhom swiveled around and

called, "Hielkje, is Miss Carter-White not down yet?"

"You can see she's not."

Gavin thumped his script and Hielkje said, "Oh!" and hastily flipped her folder open. She managed to dip the bottom of it in a fruit plate.

"I think," Reggie said loudly, "that is the opening line in Gavin's opus."

Gavin turned to glare at the singer and Hielkje cleared her throat. "I believe, sir, the lady is still abed," she read, spacing her words.

"Perhaps," Gavin said, without consulting his script, "you had better check on her."

"Yes, sir. It will be faster if I use the lift—" Raising puzzled eyes, Hielkje said in her normal voice, "Gavin, we don't have a *lift*."

He ran his fingers through his unruly hair. "Can't you read, you idiot? In brackets, after 'lift.'"

She wiped peach juice off the page. "Dumbwaiter." She cleared her throat. "Yes, sir. It will be faster if I use the dumbwaiter."

Reggie made a muffled sound and Gavin spat. "Lift! The goddamn lift. Never mind, go on."

"Make your exit and wait in the hall for a few minutes," she mumbled, and followed the instructions.

Leaning back in his chair, Gavin wiped at his brow. Despite the cool air he was sweating. He asked his wife, "Where in hell is that . . ."

Nancy shrugged and his voice trailed off. "Take it easy," she told him. "You're getting too tense. He'll be along."

"He was supposed to be right here and you know it. I tell you, Nan, he's up to something and—Ah, Hielkje, did you wake Miss Carter-White?"

A more relaxed-looking Hielkje had returned. "I think you had better come, sir," she read in a flat voice. "There appears to be a dead body in the dumbwaiter—"

"Lift!" Gavin roared.

Miss Sanderson, her shoulders shaking, put down her sandwich. Reggie muttered in her ear, "I must be mad, but I'm beginning to enjoy this."

Gavin was looking expectantly at Mrs. Montrose and that lady said in ringing tones, "I strongly suspect, Mr. Lebonhom, that this play is foul!"

"Foul play!" he shrieked. "For God's sake, read it again!"

Mrs. Montrose looked affronted but obediently read, "I strongly suspect, Mr. Lebonhom, that this is foul play."

Reggie wiped tears from streaming eyes. "She was right the *first* time."

Miss Sanderson dug a sharp elbow into his ribs. "Gavin's glaring at you. I think you're on."

Paper rustled and Reggie blurted, "I think, Mr. Lebonhom, we had better have a look in that dumb—that lift."

"That," said Alice Caspari, "is a good idea. Hielkje, are you certain the person in the lift is dead? Could it not be a seizure of some kind?"

Alice must have read her lines correctly because Gavin gave her a look of pure gratitude. He said earnestly, "Yes, Hielkje, do explain. What made you think the body is dead?"

Hielkje seemed to have lost her place. She flipped pages rapidly. "There is blood all over, sir, all over her lovely white negligee. In her back is a jeweled dagger. I saw that dagger, sir, on her dressing table when I cleaned her room. Yes, Mr. Lebonhom, Miss Carter-White is definitely in bed."

"Dead! You flaming moronic cretin. You—" Nancy put a hand on her husband's arm, he took a deep breath, and said hoarsely, "Stage direction, Hielkje."

Hielkje raised her brown eyes. "'Faint'? Gavin, should I fall on the floor—"

"Collapse on a chair. Any chair." Gavin turned to his wife. "I should never have given her such a large part. She hasn't even bothered to read through the bloody script."

"Shh, darling. She's doing her best. She's sick."

"She's making *me* sick. Collapse, Hielkje, that you should have no problem with."

Hielkje promptly obeyed, throwing her heavy body on the nearest chair, which squeaked in protest. She seemed better at action than dialogue and sagged forward across the table in a most realistic manner. Stifling an impulse to applaud, Miss Sanderson gazed around. Mrs. Montrose was devouring a sandwich, Omar had dozed off, and Alice bent her mousy head over the flashing steel needles. Fran was leaning against the sideboard, sipping coffee.

"Fran," the harried author prompted.

She put down her cup and reached for the water pitcher. Pouring into a glass, she said, "I will give her a sip of water, sir. She has had a shock."

Carrying the glass in one hand, her script in the other, she hurried across the room. Gavin was nodding approval when Fran's ankle turned, and she lurched forward and delivered the contents of the glass over Hielkje's head and shoulders. With an outraged shriek the other woman jerked upright, and Gavin tore at his hair with both hands. Reggie had given up and sprawled across his table in what seemed to be hysterics.

"I'm sorry, Gavin. These damn shoes! I told you I hadn't worn heels this high in years." Scooping up a napkin, Fran swiped at the cook's face.

Her employer seemed speechless, and Nancy said soothingly, "Darling, it will be better when we get to the next part. Fran, do carry on, please."

Dropping the napkin, Fran consulted her script. "The

sip of water did revive her, sir. She is now able to show us the dreadful thing she found." She helped the sodden cook up and immediately staggered and grabbed the woman's thick arm. Muttering a curse, Fran kicked off both sandals.

Gavin now seemed numb. He mumbled, "Mr. Knight is correct. We will all have a look in the lift. Come along."

Nudging her cat awake, Mrs. Montrose led him past Miss Sandersons' table. Her script was stuck under an arm and she was nibbling another sandwich. Alice stowed away her knitting and tagged along behind. Reggie heaved himself up. "Abigail, Mrs. Montrose is a lady with much control. If I'd kept on eating through that opening scene, I'd have choked to death. I hope the next part runs smoothly, or I'm going to get a hernia from smothering my guffaws."

"Smothering! You sounded like a bull moose at mating time."

"I'm beginning to see why Gavin has never published."

"Mystery may not be his forte. Perhaps he should try comedy."

"If he did, he'd have a best-seller." Touching her arm, he pointed. "Behold, the dead body taking nourishment."

One of the doors to the public bar was ajar, and Miss Sanderson glimpsed Dolly Carter-White. She was perched on a barstool eating her lunch from a tray. She was wearing a fuzzy scarlet jumpsuit that was as form fitting as the white silk had been. "I should have thought she'd be curled up on the dumbwaiter posing as a corpse."

"Not so," Reggie told her. "Too messy for that lovely lady. Fran told me, in strictest confidence, the part of the corpse is being played by a mannequin." He chuckled. "A dummy in a dumbwaiter. Not bad, eh?"

"I wonder where her fiancé is?"

"Probably up to no good. Must remember there's a joker loose in the Jester."

"Gavin should have had you write his play. You have a

certain way with words. Blimey, but I hope Felix isn't planning to ruin Gavin's play."

"Little late for that, Abigail. Fran and Hielkje, with Mrs. Montrose's able assistance, have handled that." He swung open a baize door. "Act one, scene two. The corpse in the lift-dumbwaiter."

Gavin, his color high and looking more cheerful, had taken up a post to the left of the stove. At his side a sulky looking Hielkje was trying to dry the bodice of her dress with a dish towel. Behind them were the wide double doors of the dumbwaiter. At that moment they were tightly closed. Alice, Mrs. Montrose and Omar, Nancy Lebonhom, and Fran were clustered around the host and his cook. Fran was standing on one leg like a stork, rubbing a black-net-covered foot against the calf of the other leg. Although the kitchen was warm with heat pulsing from the cooking stove, the stone floor must have been icy.

Waving the latecomers closer, Gavin declaimed, "Slide back the lift door, Hielkje. Don't be afraid, I'm right at your side."

Looking even more sullen, the cook grabbed both knobs and pulled the doors wide. Glaring at her master, Hielkje snarled, "There Miss Carter-White is, sir. I can't bear to look at her."

Instead of looking into the dumbwaiter, Gavin stared at his audience and said with great feeling, "By Jove, you are right! And the weapon that killed her is her jeweled dagger." Without looking away from his audience, he pointed a dramatic finger and gasped, "She has been murdered."

Someone gave a nervous titter and Miss Sanderson tried to see over Fran's shoulder. That shoulder went rigid. At the same moment Gavin swung around and looked down into the dumbwaiter. In a low, venomous voice he said, "Damn it to hell. Had to do it, didn't you? First ruin me, now ruin my poor play. Well . . . you've done it. Joke's over. Get the hell up."

Reggie hissed in Miss Sanderson's ear, "Sounds like Felix has struck again."

Miss Sanderson felt a stirring of pity for the beleaguered Gavin Lebonhom. She must try to rescue something from this debacle. Pushing at Fran's back, she ad-libbed, "I'm a detective. Let me through. Stand aside."

There was a ripple of movement and the other guests cleared a path. Stepping up beside Hielkje, Miss Sanderson looked down. The platform was long and wide and came to her waist. On it a figure sprawled. It was face down with the legs drawn up and the right hand, palm up, at its side. The other arm was tucked up under the chest. Chestnut hair spilled over the collar of a tweed jacket. From the back of that jacket an ebony handle protruded. Tiny gold letters caught a glint of light and sparkled.

Gavin was now raving and cursing Felix Caspari. Some of the others were giggling. Miss Sanderson said curtly, "Shut up." She put down a hand and gingerly touched the inert hand on the splintery boards. The flesh felt like cold wax.

Turning, Hielkje bent to have a look. Then she gave a soft sigh and crumpled to the stone floor. This time her faint was done even more artistically than the one she had counterfeited in the dining room.

CHAPTER NINE

NO ATTENTION WAS PAID TO THE UNCONSCIOUS COOK. Everyone was gaping at the still figure on the dumbwaiter. Miss Sanderson said, "Fran," and the woman stepped forward and shoved Mrs. Montrose to one side. She bent over Felix Caspari, her hands moving swiftly and competently. Then she straightened and pulled the doors closed. "We aren't acting any further. He's dead."

Dropping her knitting bag, Alice burst into tears. Gavin covered his face with both hands, and his wife had turned a sickly green. Alice was swaying and Reggie pulled up a chair and lowered her into it. He asked Fran, "Are you certain?"

"He's already starting to cool."

Clapping a hand over her mouth, Nancy sprinted to the sink. Bending over it, she retched. Mrs. Montrose dropped her cat's leash and dampened a dishcloth. She patted the girl's heaving shoulders and clapped the towel over her brow. Both Fran and Reggie were staring at Miss Sanderson. The secretary decided she must start playing her role in earnest. "All of you but Fran get out of here," she ordered. "Gavin and Reggie, you'll have to carry Hielkje. Mrs. Montrose, you take Alice and Nancy along."

Reggie nudged Gavin, and they bent and hoisted Hielkje up between them. Her head lolled back and Gavin grunted, "She weighs a ton."

Mrs. Montrose pulled Nancy away from the sink. "Someone must break this to Dolly."

"I'll do it." Alice pulled herself up and picked up her knitting bag. Tears were pouring down her face, but there was a faint note of satisfaction in her voice. "It's *my* place to do it. I'm Felix's widow."

The Widow Caspari was the first to exit the kitchen. Gavin and Reggie, panting over the cook's supine body, were last. Omar, dragging his leash, tripped Gavin, and he muttered a number of four-letter words.

As the baize doors swung into place, Fran turned and asked, "What do we do?"

"Get on to the police, of course. But first—have you any idea how long he's been dead?"

"I'm not a doctor."

"You're the closest we have to one at this moment."

"At a guess I'd say at least a couple of hours."

"Hmm. That would put it about eleven-thirty. Shortly before we had lunch."

"It's only a guess. The postmortem will pin it down fairly close."

Miss Sanderson led the way to the lobby and closed the doors to the public bar. A gust of wind rocked the front door of the inn, followed by a wild shriek from the direction of the bar. Fran winced. "Sounds like the widow has broken the news to the fiancée." She shivered and muttered, "Better get something on my feet before I get pneumonia."

Miss Sanderson headed toward the desk, and Fran fished around in a closet and found a pair of high rubber boots. As she tugged them on, she called, "Finchley is closest. Ask for Inspector James."

Miss Sanderson held out the receiver. "Dead."

"It can't be. Reggie was using it this morning." Taking the receiver, she held it to an ear and jiggled the bar. "Well, it's not working now."

"Could the storm—"

"Might have. Last winter during a storm like this the phone was out for a couple of days." She circled the bar and bent out of sight. When she rose, she held the end of a cord in her hand. "Not the storm. It's been cut."

The two women stared at each other. Miss Sanderson said, "What about the boat? Can you get to the mainland in this storm?"

Fran trotted over and opened the front door. The wind drove sleet into her face and nearly ripped the door from her hand. She struggled to close the door, and Miss Sanderson ran to help. Before it shut she saw white-tipped waves battering at the pier. "What do you think, Fran?"

The lace cap bobbed as Fran shook her head. "It's risky. Too heavy seas for a boat that size, even for a short distance. Under ordinary circumstances I wouldn't try it, but these are hardly ordinary. I'll give it a go. First, I better get these damn clothes off." She headed for the hall.

Miss Sanderson called after her, "Someone had better go with you."

"Who would you suggest?"

"One of the men."

"Gavin's hopeless. Probably gets seasick in the tub. But Reggie seems to have a cool head. Rout him out. Warn him it's dangerous. There are boots and waterproofs in that closet."

Miss Sanderson opened a door and peered into the bar. It looked like a battlefield. Hielkje was stretched out on a bench with a pillow under her head and her feet propped up. The widow was sitting under the watercolor, collapsed over the table, her face buried in her knitting bag. Dolly didn't look as much like a Barbie doll. Her creamy hair was hanging over a damp face with smudged makeup, and Mrs. Montrose was holding a glass to her lips. Omar was perched on the polished counter, nonchalantly washing his face with a fluffy gray paw. Beside the cat, Gavin perched on a stool, but he didn't seem to notice the cat or anything else. His wife had her back turned and appeared to be retching in the bar sink.

Catching Reggie's eyes, Miss Sanderson jerked her head toward the foyer. She explained the situation and then said, "You'll have to volunteer. Fran says it's risky. Do you know anything about boats?"

"Haven't the foggiest, but I'm a quick study." He burrowed into the closet, and by the time Fran had returned, he'd pulled an oilskin over his parka and located rubber boots. He tugged his toque down over his ears.

Fran eyed him doubtfully and pulled an oilskin over her pea jacket. As she jammed the watch cap down over her head, she asked, "Did Abigail mention that the boat could capsize?"

"She hinted at it. You do have life jackets I presume."

"Of course. But they'll be as much help as snowballs in hell if we're thrown into that water."

"Thanks. I needed that."

"All ready?"

"Ready, but far from eager. Let's go." He squeezed Miss Sanderson's arm. "Bear up. We'll be as quick as we can."

She told him shakily, "Reggie, I take back what I said about chivalry having vanished."

This time she had to fight to close the heavy door by herself. She glimpsed them struggling down the rocky path. Fran nearly fell, and Reggie grabbed her. Miss Sanderson shook a worried head. This was lunacy. They shouldn't try it. But they were both levelheaded, and if it

103

looked hopeless, they would give it up and return to the inn.

Time to test her own courage by going into the bar. She decided not to tell the others about the severed telephone cord. They would panic. She straightened her thin shoulders and opened the door, trying to look confident. Mrs. Montrose was now trying to drain brandy into Hielkje's slack mouth. La Montrose, Miss Sanderson thought, was not only the oldest person there but the most composed. Heads swiveled toward the door, and Mrs. Montrose snapped, "How long will the police be?"

"I don't know. The telephone is out of order."

"What are we going to do?" Nancy threw down the damp towel and her voice rose with a raw edge of hysteria.

"It's being done. Fran and Reggie are taking the boat across to the cars. It won't take long for them to drive in to Finchley."

"Thank God for the boat," Gavin mumbled.

Alice jumped to her feet and the bag tumbled off the table, spilling purple wool and glittering needles. "Reggie? Reggie's leaving here?"

"To summon the police," Miss Sanderson said. "Fran couldn't go alone."

"He's escaping: He killed my husband! He hated Felix, blamed him for his brother's death."

"*Alice.*" Mrs. Montrose thumped down the glass. "Control yourself."

The widow turned on her. "If it wasn't Reggie, it was you."

"Just why would I kill Felix?"

"Because of Sonny. You always blamed Felix for Sonny."

"Don't be ridiculous. And stop making wild accusations." Mrs. Montrose paused and then made one of her own. "The police may feel *you* had an excellent motive for wanting your husband dead."

"Me? But I love . . . loved him."

"And there's your motive. Rather than lose him you might have decided you'd rather see him dead."

Felix's patron and his widow were glaring like Bengal tigers. "Both of you settle down," Miss Sanderson said. "Save your strength. You're going to need it."

Some Dutch courage may increase my own strength, Miss Sanderson thought, flipping up the panel in the counter. She took down a brandy bottle and poured a generous tot. The door to the foyer banged open and two bedraggled figures staggered in. Their oilskins dripped water, and Fran's ponytail clung damply to her neck. Heading toward the counter, they stretched out hands. Miss Sanderson promptly filled those beseeching hands with brandy glasses. "You decided not to try?" she asked.

Brushing a sodden ringlet away from his cheek, Reggie panted, "Someone decided for us."

"Used an ax and stove in the bottom of the boat," Fran explained breathlessly.

Gavin swung around and his eyes finally focused. "Exactly what happened to the telephone?"

"The cord was cut," Reggie said.

They panicked. Dolly came bolting out of the alcove, Hielkje let out a bellow and nearly fell off the bench, Nancy proceeded to have hysterics. Mrs. Montrose again rose to the occasion and cracked her palm across Nancy's face. Following the older woman's example, Miss Sanderson slapped her own hand on the counter. "Stop it! Stop it this instant. Losing your heads won't help."

"We're marooned," Gavin quavered. "Cut off from help with a murderer among us. We're all going to be murdered!"

"Keep that up and I'll oblige you right now," Reggie

105

told him. "Listen. Abigail's right. We're *not* marooned. There's the causeway. As soon as the storm slackens, we'll cross to the mainland. At low tide, of course. Right, Fran?"

"If you happen to have suicidal impulses," she said, and refreshed her drink. "I must have, because when the storm dies down, I'll give it a go."

"You see," Miss Sanderson said. "It's only a matter of carrying on until the weather clears."

Hielkje seemed to be feeling somewhat better. She pulled herself up into a sitting position and said brightly, "Last winter a storm like this lasted for a week."

Nancy wailed and then subsided as Mrs. Montrose lifted a threatening hand. Pulling off the oilskin, Reggie draped it over a stool. "Hielkje, you're a great little help. Anyway, the weather is out of our hands. Fran says there's lots of food and enough fuel, so we'll muddle through. Right now I vote our detective get to work."

All eyes swung hopefully to Miss Sanderson. With a sinking heart she told them, "I'm a legal secretary, not a detective."

Giving her a wry grin, Fran repeated what the older woman had said in the kitchen. "At this moment you're the closest to one that we have."

Miss Sanderson lifted her chin. "Very well, I'll try. Now, about the mannequin that was supposed to be in the dumbwaiter. Who was supposed to put it there?" Fran raised a hand and the secretary asked, "When?"

"I did it after Gavin and I finished hauling coal in. That was . . ."

"We started at seven," Gavin said. "Finished up at exactly eight minutes after nine. I was watching the clock."

"I'll bet you were," Fran said. "When we'd finished I washed up, and then Gavin called to me and told me to fix up the mannequin in the dumbwaiter. I told him there was

. 106

loads of time but he insisted, and I went up to the attic and did it." She paused. "Want to look around up there, Abigail?"

There was nothing Miss Sanderson wanted less, but she followed the younger woman through the lobby and up the staircase. "Better explain the layout of this floor, Fran."

"That's the VIP suite used by Felix. Two rooms and bath with only one door opening into the sitting room. Directly opposite that door is Nancy's sitting room, then the Lebonhoms' bedroom, then Gavin's study. All three rooms connected by interior doors. My room is beside Gavin's study, and Hielkje's is next to Felix's suite. The lav and bath are down this branch hall, and at the end is a door leading to the steps Gavin had boxed in." She swung open a door and Miss Sanderson saw a landing painted Chinese red with steps leading upward. "Now, Abigail, back to the main hall, and there is the staircase leading to the attic. Watch yourself, these steps are steep and narrow."

It was more a ladder than a staircase, and as they climbed, the air got progressively colder. When they reached the top, Miss Sanderson decided that the lower regions of the Jester were, in comparison, positively balmy. She tugged her cardigan closer and listened to Fran's rapid explanation. "Those are the doors of the dumbwaiter. The four doors opposite lead to storerooms and a lav no longer in operation. Originally this floor must have been used as quarters for the servants. Poor devils weren't exactly swaddled in luxury." She opened the door directly across from the dumbwaiter. "This is the room Gavin fitted up for his mannequins. Sort of a prop room. At first he planned to have the guest playing the part of the victim pose as the corpse, but Nancy talked him out of it. Said she didn't think Dolores Carter-White would agree to being crammed onto that platform and having her clothes covered with red ink—God!"

She had nearly tripped over a figure sprawled on the floor. The woman had long creamy blond hair and a jeweled hilt protruded from its back. The white silk was soaked with what looked like blood.

"Sorry," Fran said shakily. "I fixed it up myself, but it looks real, doesn't it?"

"A dead ringer for Dolly. Give me the details, Fran."

"After I spoke to Gavin, I came up here and dressed it." She wa·ed toward a rack of clothing. Propped up against it, three other mannequins, two male and one female, stared with glassy eyes. On a bench beside them a number of wigs sat on holders.

Miss Sanderson's eyes ranged around the room. "Gavin did a thorough job on his theatrics."

"He got the stuff fairly cheaply from a shop going out of business. Anyway, I stuck the dagger in the back of the dummy, dribbled ink on it, and pulled it out here." She stepped across the hall and opened the doors of the dumbwaiter. "I arranged it on the platform and then let the dumbwaiter down to kitchen level."

Poking her head in the hole, Miss Sanderson looked at the system of cables and then bent forward. This part of the dumbwaiter was, like the kitchen opening, waist high. No danger of falling. She peered down into a black well. An icy current of air stirred her hair. At the bottom the earthly remains of Felix Caspari, master chef, huddled, separated from the kitchen by flimsy doors.

Fran must have been following the older woman's thoughts. "Neither Hielkje nor Nancy will go into the kitchen with . . ."

"We'd better bring him up." She turned away from the black well. "It's going to be heavy. Think we can handle it?"

"Stand aside. I can do it." Reaching up, Fran made an adjustment. "This thing was in bad shape when I came here. I had to completely overhaul it. Installed new cables and replaced the old platform with a larger one."

"What do you use it for?"

"Mainly for fuel for the bedroom floor. Believe it or not, but there are seven fireplaces to keep going on that floor. But"—she gave a heave and started to crank—"I've even used it to move furniture. Ah, here it comes."

All Miss Sanderson could hear was a muted rumble. "It moves quietly."

"I keep it well oiled. And if you're thinking it could be hauled up and down without being heard, you're right."

Looking over Fran's shoulder, Miss Sanderson could now discern the shadowy shape of the platform. She braced herself. Then the platform was there and Fran locked it into position. She started to close the doors, but Miss Sanderson stopped her. "We'll have to take him out of there."

"Should we? Won't the police—"

"The police aren't here and we don't know when they will be. Fran, I know it's asking a lot, but I can't do it alone. We have to . . . to look him over."

For a moment Fran stood indecisively. Finally she nodded and her ponytail bobbed. "There are a couple of spare doors in the boxroom. Last fall I replaced the ones on my room and Hielkje's. We can use one as a stretcher."

They retrieved the door and placed it on the floor. Fran gave brisk instructions. "You take his legs. I'll handle his shoulders. Lord, he's stiffening up. Heave!"

They swung the grisly object off the platform, nearly dropped it, and then lowered it carefully to the door. Miss Sanderson stood back panting. "He must weigh over two hundred."

"Big man." Fran bent and grasped one end of the door. "You lift the other end, Abigail. We'll put this in with the mannequins."

They lowered the door in front of the clothes rack. As

Miss Sanderson sank to her knees, she felt as though the glassy eyes of the three mannequins were watching her. She rolled the stiff figure back, and Fran braced it from the other side. Felix's eyes were wide open and his mouth gaped. From the corner of that mouth a worm of dried blood had seeped into his short beard. Tearing her eyes from that face, Miss Sanderson pulled the jacket clear of the barrel-like chest. "No blood on his shirt."

"No exit wound," Fran said calmly. "The knife is imbedded in his chest. Internal bleeding, and any blood from the entrance wound is soaked up by his shirt and this heavy jacket." Bending forward, she mercifully closed the staring eyes.

They eased him back on his face and Miss Sanderson studied the tweed-clad back. The ebony hilt protruded from between the shoulder blades. On it, tiny initials—FGC— sparkled. Custom-made for murder, she thought, and her eyes closed. Fran asked, "Abigail, are you all right?"

"Barely," she whispered, as Fran took her arm and hauled her to her feet. "Fine detective. But this is the first time I've actually handled . . ."

"I know. Takes a bit of getting used to. Take deep breaths."

Miss Sanderson took deep breaths and steadied. She forced herself back to her knees and ran her finger over the tweed. A fingernail snagged and she said, "Take a look at this."

"A rip?"

"I don't think so. Looks as though it was cut. No jagged edges."

Fran examined the fabric. "A slit about an inch and a half long. About midway between the knife wound and the right armpit. Over a shoulder blade. Only the tweed cut; the lining's intact."

110

Miss Sanderson stood up. "Is there anything up here we can use to cover him?"

"A set of discarded curtains. I'll get one."

They draped the door and its burden with a rose-colored curtain. The velvet was faded and worn and dust billowed up from its folds. Miss Sanderson was thankful to leave the mannequin room and the staring glassy eyes. They stopped on the lower floor to wash up, and as Fran toweled her hands off, her companion perched on the edge of a claw-footed tub, her thumbnail beating a tattoo against a front tooth.

For once she wasn't asked what she was doing. Instead, Fran said, "When I think, I tug at my hair. Want to share?"

"That slit, deliberately cut. The positioning of it. What does it suggest?"

"I haven't the slightest idea." Fran's level brows drew together. "All I can say is, Felix Caspari was not a man to wear a damaged jacket. If he'd known it—"

"Oh, Felix knew all about that slit." Lifting cool blue eyes, Miss Sanderson smiled grimly. "He cut the slit himself. The last joke was played on the practical joker."

CHAPTER TEN

A CERTAIN SERENITY HAD RETURNED TO THE PUBLIC bar. Hielkje Visser had changed from her maid's costume and now looked like a sausage stuffed into a plaid shirt and jeans. Dolly had repaired her makeup and fluffed out her Barbie doll hair. The Widow Caspari was working on the dreadful purple wool. Omar had gone to sleep on the counter, and Reggie, swinging long legs, was perched on a stool near him. Nancy was huddled on a bench near the fire, and Miss Sanderson noticed the girl's color was better. Miss Sanderson checked her watch. Thirty-eight after three. Slightly over two hours since the discovery of the murder and it seemed like ten years. The room was shadowed and Gavin was moving around, lighting lamps, pulling curtains over windows, as though trying to shut out the storm. The sight of sleet slashing against glass disappeared, but the wind howled under the eaves and moaned against the hidden glass.

Reggie jumped up and offered brandy or beer, but Miss Sanderson shook her head. "Nancy, you and Hielkje make coffee. Reggie, the bar's closed. We need clear heads."

Reggie nodded. "Better rustle up some food too. I'm starving."

112

Setting down a lamp with a thud, Gavin pointed a dramatic finger. "Thinking of food with Felix in the kitchen stiff and stark."

"Fasting won't help Felix," Mrs. Montrose pointed out.

Nancy whimpered and Hielkje said, "I am not putting a foot in the kitchen. Not with that thing in the lift."

"Wonder of wonders," Reggie said. "She finally got her line right."

"The dumbwaiter is no longer in the kitchen," Fran told the two women. "It's now in the attic. Come along, I'll give you a hand."

Miss Sanderson climbed onto a stool and waited until a serving wagon was wheeled in and coffee and cheese rolls were distributed. Apparently Gavin had overcome his squeamishness as he helped himself generously. Even the widow managed to eat. The only ones with no appetite were Fran Hornblower and Miss Sanderson.

Gavin chewed, swallowed, and reached for the creamer. "And has the great detective come to any conclusions?" There was a sneer in his voice.

"I know how the murder was done," she told him. "But the identity of the murderer . . . who he or she is—"

"If you say X, I'll be sick," Gavin told her. "It's trite."

"This isn't one of your lousy scripts," Reggie said hotly. "This is real, so drop the great-writer bit."

Gavin flushed and Miss Sanderson asked him, "In your play, what was *your* murderer called?"

"The Jester."

"Aha!" Mrs. Montrose leaned forward, her simian face splitting into a smile. "A Freudian slip. And I'll wager Felix was cast as the Jester."

Gavin was now close to the color of Alice Caspari's knitting. Disregarding him, Miss Sanderson said, "Jester will serve. Now, we'll go back to yesterday morning.

113

Gavin, Fran said you accused her of opening a window in your study."

"Either she did or Nan did. Neither of them would admit it." Gavin turned on his wife. "That was sheer carelessness. Leaving that door to our bedroom unlocked. I've warned you repeatedly about that."

"Papers on your desk were disarranged?" Miss Sanderson asked.

"Blown all over the place. Even some sheets on the floor. The window had been closed again, but I could tell at a glance what had happened."

"Were these papers your script?"

"My master script. Everything was there, including a synopsis of the murder, how the mannequin was to be arranged on the dumbwaiter—" He stopped and his eyes widened. "Felix!"

"Exactly. While you were occupied helping bring in the coal, Felix got into your study and read your script. This morning he waited for Fran to finish in the attic—"

"You're right!" Fran jerked forward. "After I finished in the attic I was passing Felix's suite, and he popped out and asked how things were coming. I told him swimmingly and—"

"And he knew the coast was clear." Miss Sanderson lit a cigarette and gazed at the cloud of bluish smoke. "Felix must already have decided exactly how he was going to make Gavin look ridiculous. He must have cut a slit in the back of his jacket, and he took one of his knives . . . Gavin, come over here. Turn so the others can see your back. Now, Gavin is wearing a jacket similar to Felix's. On the dead man's the slit is right about here." She drew a finger down the rough tweed and felt Gavin's back muscles quivering. "The reason Felix cut into an expensive jacket is clear. The slit was intended to be a pocket to push the knife in, so at a casual glance it would look as though the hilt

114

was sticking out of his back. But he ran into difficulty and had to ring in a confederate to help."

Reggie jumped off the counter for a closer look. "Why would Felix have needed help?"

"Hand me one of those swizzle sticks, Reggie. Now, Gavin, take this in your left hand and try to position it as though the pocket is right where my finger is resting."

He wriggled and twisted. "Can't be done."

"Ah," Reggie said. "A flaw in your reasoning, Abigail. Felix could have stuck the knife in the slit *before* he put the jacket on."

"No." It was Alice who spoke. "My late husband's knives were always honed razor sharp. He could have cut himself putting his jacket on. Felix would never have done that."

"Precisely," Miss Sanderson said. "And if Felix had cut himself, the joke would have been on him, not on Gavin. He found someone willing to help play the trick, and they sneaked up to the attic to prepare the scene. The mannequin was lifted off the platform, and Felix climbed onto it and handed his confederate the knife. Then he waited for it to be artistically tucked into the slit." She took a deep breath. "But the joker had unfortunately chosen the Jester. The Jester ignored the slit and drove the knife deep into Felix's back. Then the Jester lowered the platform again to the kitchen—"

"One moment," Mrs. Montrose interrupted. "Wouldn't that have taken a great deal of strength?"

Turning, Fran ran her eyes down Mrs. Montrose's frail body. "You could have done it. The way I've rigged the cables it would have been simple and easy. And it moves quietly. Abigail noticed that."

Gavin shoved his cup away so violently that it tipped and brown fluid flowed across the counter. "That bastard! First he ruins me, then he tries to ruin my play. I suppose

115

he was going to jump up and laugh and shout something funny!"

"Gavin!" his wife cried. "He's *dead*."

"Then he's a *dead* bastard."

The Black Knight ignored Gavin's outburst. "The telephone. I used it at . . . let's see, it must have been—Fran, you came into the foyer while I was speaking with my manager. Any idea of the time?"

"I'd just finished in the attic. It was about—"

"The time doesn't matter," Miss Sanderson said flatly. "That foyer is so cold no one lingers in it. Anytime after Felix was killed the Jester could have slipped in there and cut the cord."

"Only between the time of the murder and the time we all were together in the dining room," Alice said rather shrewdly. "The only person who wasn't in the dining room was . . ." She pointed a knitting needle at Dolly.

"And also Hielkje," Mrs. Montrose pointed out. "Remember, she left the dining room and shut the door."

Hielkje tugged at her plaid shirt and said indignantly, "I simply waited outside the door for a few moments."

"Quite long enough to have cut through the cord," Mrs. Montrose told her.

"This is a lesson in futility," Miss Sanderson said. "That cord could have been cut by any one of us before we gathered in the dining room."

"What about checking alibis?" Fran asked.

"Futile again. There are three entrances to the attic. From the main floor, from the guest wing, and a set of outside steps at the back of the inn. In a place this size it would have been easy to slip up there and back undetected. Unless two people were together constantly from about ten this morning until noon."

Brows furrowed in thought and eight heads shook. "You see," Miss Sanderson said, "I have no alibi either. I was

alone in my room until Reggie came to get me for lunch-
eon. I could have slipped up that boxed-in staircase to the
attic and no one would have been the wiser."

Reggie nodded. "I could have too. I saw Gavin when he
brought coal into my room and spoke briefly with Fran in
the lobby after I'd finished my call, but that's it. What
about the boat, Abigail?"

"No doubt done during the night. The noise from the
storm would have covered any sounds the Jester made
leaving the inn. Where was the ax kept, Fran?"

"Hanging from the wall of the boathouse. It wouldn't
have taken long to chop a hole in the boat." Fran looked at
Miss Sanderson. "But why go to these lengths? The Jester
can't hope to escape. *All* of us are marooned here. Why
delay having the police arrive?"

"There can be only one reason for that."

It was so quiet that all that could be heard was the shriek
of the wind and a shutter banging. Slowly, sick comprehension showed on the faces of every person in the room
with the exception of one. Gavin, his expression puzzled,
looked from face to face. Hielkje dropped her cup to the
floor and it splintered to pieces. It was Alice Caspari who
whispered, "Because the Jester hasn't finished. He's planning on another victim."

"Or *victims*," Gavin blurted, and then proceeded to
splinter into as many pieces as the china cup had.

"Brace up!" Marching over, Mrs. Montrose stood before him. He towered over her. "Stop that or you'll get
what I gave your wife."

Reggie cursed and shoved Gavin onto the bench where
Alice Caspari sat, her knitting neglected in her lap. The
man crumpled down beside her, and over their heads, in
Noel Canard's watercolor, the distorted figure holding an
ax still watched the tiny skaters.

117

Her eyes locked on her father's painting, Nancy said hoarsely, "*Father*. He's the Jester."

Which proves, Miss Sanderson thought dolefully, that I'm about as good at therapy as I am at detecting. "Nancy, the only people on this island are in this room." Robby, she called silently, where are you in my hour of need? The answer was evident. In chambers going bonkers from overwork while she was going rapidly bonkers trapped in this inn with a group of people either in shock or having raving hysterics. She looked around for support and found it. Fran and Reggie had pulled themselves together, and Dolly's porcelain face was a serene oval.

"Abigail is correct," Fran said firmly. "Nancy, there are only two outbuildings—the boathouse and the coal shed. I promise you, anyone foolish enough to hide in them would die from exposure."

"I mean *here*. Somewhere in the inn. Hiding. He's mad, I tell you, mad!"

Hielkje gave a convulsive shudder and Gavin glanced apprehensively at the door leading to the lobby. Fran threw her hands up, and both she and Reggie looked at Miss Sanderson.

There was only one thing to do and Miss Sanderson proceeded to do it. "Nancy, we'll search the inn and the guest wing and prove to you once and for all that Noel Canard is *not* here. Fran, you and Gavin take the attic—"

"Not me." Gavin's head shook so violently that his mustache danced over his upper lip. "I am not setting foot out of this room."

Darting the man a contemptuous look, Dolly came gracefully to her feet. "I'll go with Fran."

Miss Sanderson said, "Reggie, you take this floor and the guest wing with . . ."

Mrs. Montrose stood up and tugged her quilted vest down. "I'll accompany Reggie."

"Good." Walking over, Miss Sanderson tapped Nancy's shoulder. "You'll help me search the bedroom floor and no arguments. We'll also lock all the exterior doors and the three entrances to that boxed-in staircase. Where are the keys?"

"We've never locked up," Fran said. "But there must be a ring of keys. Right, Hielkje?"

"In the kitchen. In the back of the drawer where the dish towels are kept."

Fran brought the keys and started distributing them. "They're labeled. Here's your lot, Reggie. Abigail, you take these." She tucked the rest in the pocket of her pea jacket.

Leaving Gavin, Alice, and Hielkje in the bar, the teams set out. Reggie paused to light the lamp on the desk in the lobby and then grinned down at Mrs. Montrose. "We'll check the dining room first. Nervous?"

She smiled up at him. "Not in the slightest." Thrusting a hand in the pocket of her red vest, she pulled out a small object and held it up. "Felix never traveled without his knives, and I always have my derringer with me. My husband gave it to me shortly after our marriage, and it's either in my handbag or pocket or, at night, under my pillow."

"How pretty," Dolly said. "The handle is set with mother-of-pearl."

Reggie laughed. "And how ferocious. A charming toy."

"Mock if you wish," Mrs. Montrose said, "but at close range this little toy will kill."

Reggie bowed to her. "In that case you go first and protect me."

They went to the hall for flashlights, and then Fran and Dolly preceded Miss Sanderson and Nancy up the staircase. Fran stopped to light the lamp at the top, and then her companion and she disappeared into the blackness of the hall.

"Where will we start?" Nancy asked in a quaking voice.

Terrified, Miss Sanderson thought, but with more courage than her husband was showing. "Right here. Felix's suite."

The chef's suite was totally different from the rest of the inn. It was furnished in a lavish modern manner. When the lamps were lit, they displayed a sitting room, bedroom, and bath decorated with pale blues and dove gray. The sole touch of vivid color was an abstract over the mantel. It too was modern, with swirls and blobs of reds, ambers, greens. On a chest were several decanters, an array of glasses, a pigskin case. Miss Sanderson lifted the top of the handsome case and eyed the one indentation. Felix's favorite knife, the one with the six-inch blade, was missing. Well, she knew the location of that. While Nancy remained in the sitting room, the older woman checked the bedroom and bath. She poked around in the huge wardrobe and found only an assortment of tailor-made suits, a row of expensive shoes, a set of pigskin luggage. Draped over a chair was the creamy Aran sweater that Felix had been wearing when she met him.

In comparison with the luxury of the VIP suite, Nancy's sitting room and the bedroom she shared with her husband were shabby. Gavin's study was better furnished. He had a handsome desk and an onyx-and-silver desk set, a typewriter on a side table, two walls lined with books. Over the mantel another watercolor hung. Miss Sanderson glanced at it. For a moment it looked cheerful and innocent. It showed a beach scene, a child building a sand castle, two other children splashing through the waves. She had no difficulty locating what she was starting to think of as the artist's trademark. Behind the children a shark's fin sliced through the water. Gruesome, innocence again threatened with horror. She noticed that Noel's daughter was studiously avoiding looking at it.

When they stepped back into the hall, Miss Sanderson selected a key and locked the door leading to Felix's suite and his set of razor-sharp knives. As she headed down the hall, Nancy was so close that she walked up Miss Sanderson's heel. Swinging around, Miss Sanderson looked into the round face and wide eyes. "You're quite safe, you know."

"I'm behaving badly, Auntie Abby."

"We're all upset and nervous, my dear, but flying to pieces isn't going to help." She rested a consoling hand on the girl's shoulder and wondered if it was the shoulder of a murderer. Looking down at that face, so much like her childhood friend's, she couldn't believe it, but then Nancy Canard had once been an actress.

They moved down the branch hall, pausing twice to shine their flashes in the lavatory and the bath. At the far end of the hall Miss Sanderson opened the door and stepped out on the landing, flashing the beam of her light first down the Chinese-red stairs, then up. As the light hit the upper landing, it caught Fran's startled face and ponytail. Both women jumped and Fran called down, "Ahoy. Nearly finished up here. How are you doing?"

"Only your room and Hielkje's to do."

"Be sure to look under the beds. Wouldn't want a nasty surprise."

As Miss Sanderson locked the door, Nancy said plaintively, "Fran's making fun of me, isn't she?"

"No. She's only trying to introduce a lighter note." Silently Miss Sanderson added, And thank the Lord for that.

Both the remaining rooms were small, bare, and contained no hiding places. After Miss Sanderson had locked the rear door leading to the exterior steps, she turned to Nancy. "You do agree there's no one up here?"

"Yes, but—"

"All clear in the attic," Dolly called.

The other two searchers, Dolly in the lead, were making their way down the narrow steps. They walked in a group back up the hall and trotted down to the lower one. There they found Reggie and Mrs. Montrose, one hand jammed in the pocket of her vest, replacing their flashlights. Reggie's white smile flashed. "Nary a monster. We checked the unfinished rooms and all the ones that are occupied. The rear door and the one to the staircase are firmly locked. Hey, any one lock the front door yet?"

"You have that key," Fran pointed out.

"So I have. Wait a moment and we'll break the good news en masse."

The people in the bar had consoled themselves with a freshly fueled fire and a fresh pot of coffee. The searchers headed directly to the serving wagon and Dolly poured coffee. She handed a cup to Miss Sanderson, and her emerald eyes ranged past the older woman and settled disdainfully on Gavin Lebonhom. The news that there was no one lurking in the building didn't seem to be reassuring him. He rubbed his chin and said, "While you were gone, I was thinking. Any of you ever read that mystery about a group of people on the isolated island? They were murdered one by one, and the murderer turned out to one of the victims who had only been pretending to be dead."

Reggie muttered a weary curse, and Fran spun around. "Are you insinuating that Felix Caspari is faking?"

"Well . . ."

"For God's sake, Gavin, stop being an utter ass! Abigail and I lifted him out of the dumbwaiter and he's not only dead but rigor mortis is setting in. If you think we're both in a conspiracy with Felix, you can go up and look at the body. He's in the mannequin room." She muttered, "And that's where you should be—among the other dummies."

122

"No need to be insulting. I'm only trying to help."

Miss Sanderson carried her steaming cup to the counter and climbed up on a stool. "That kind of help is doing more harm than good. Calm down and think constructively. If the Jester wanted to kill all of us, it would be simple."

The widow lifted her eyes from her knitting. "What do you mean?"

Miss Sanderson jerked her silver curls toward the serving wagon. "Poison in the coffee would do it."

Several cups were lowered, and Miss Sanderson lifted her own and took a drink. Dolly, casting a mocking look at Gavin, drained her cup. Gavin was gnawing at the end of his mustache. "Who is going to hold those keys? I vote Abigail does."

"You do trust me?"

"No reason not to. No motive. You only met us a couple of days ago."

"Perhaps," Reggie said in a sepulchral voice, "Abigail is a homicidal maniac with an aversion to celebrities."

Throwing back her head, Fran laughed. "Then I'm in no danger."

Miss Sanderson darted exasperated looks at them. "Act constructive and find something to put these keys in."

Folding back the counter flap, Reggie fumbled under the bar. "Got it." He pulled out a paper bag, swept the keys into it, and handed it to her. "Fran and I won't do further comedy turns. Carry on."

Miss Sanderson was tired and her head was aching dully, but she tried to carry on. "By now we're all agreed the only protection is to find the identity of the Jester. To do that I must question you about your pasts, your relationships with each other and with the murdered man. Do you agree?"

One by one heads nodded, and Mrs. Montrose said,

"I've nothing to hide, but some of that may be . . . it will be painful to relate. I will not answer questions unless it is done in private."

Fran touched Miss Sanderson's arm. "I'll haul heaters into the saloon bar. You can set up quarters there. Gavin, you come help and no excuses. I'm not carrying both of them."

Gavin went along without protest, and Reggie jerked his head at Hielkje. "You and I will rustle up a hot meal. We could all use one. And we'll serve in the kitchen. Might as well be warm."

Miss Sanderson smiled at him. "Did you once do a stint in a restaurant?"

"As a busboy, but I'm a pretty fair bachelor cook."

Miss Sanderson glanced around. "Who's my first volunteer?"

"Might as well start with me." Mrs. Montrose came over to the counter and scooped up her cat. "Alice had better be there too."

"But you said—"

"You'll soon understand, Abigail. Alice has a starring part in this. Haven't you, dear?" she asked acidly. "Did you know our Alice was once an actress? Bit parts only, so this will be a nice change for her."

Alice was stuffing her knitting into the bag. "That's how I met Blanche Waggoner. She was always hanging around the theater, and I introduced her to Sonny Montrose—"

"That's quite enough. This information is for Abigail's ears only."

Fran looked around the door. "The heaters are in place. And I put a couple of pens and a notebook on the table. Need anything else?"

"No, that's fine."

"If you need me, I'll be in the kitchen giving Reggie a

124

hand. Hielkje's comfortably ensconced in a chair watching him. Says she's too upset to work."

Miss Sanderson wondered if Fran was noticing her friend used her health as an excuse to dodge work. Hielkje certainly didn't look well, but the secretary had a hunch she traded on that appearance. Well, none of her business. Right now her business was unmasking a murderer.

In the saloon bar the heaters had been set at the ends of the refectory table and three lamps had been lit. One was on the table near a notebook and some pens. Miss Sanderson took a chair beside one heater, and Mrs. Montrose sank into the one beside the other heater. Alice Caspari glanced around and then pulled over the footstool and perched on it. She opened her knitting bag and Mrs. Montrose snapped, "Can't you leave that alone for a moment?"

"Knitting soothes my nerves, Sybil. A habit I picked up in the theater. While waiting to be called, you know."

Miss Sanderson flipped open the notebook and wondered how to begin. Mrs. Montrose took the decision out of her hands. "I'd better start from the first time I saw Felix. Don't look so glum, Abigail, I'll only give the highlights."

She marshaled her thoughts and then proceeded to give a concise account of her relationship with the dead man. Felix, it appeared, had been an illegitimate child, the son of the Montrose family's gardener's only daughter. "A loose woman," Mrs. Montrose said sternly. The loose woman had deserted her son when the child was five, and his grandfather had asked permission to raise Felix in his cottage on the Montrose estate. Mrs. Montrose was reluctant to agree.

"The boy's background," she explained. "My son was the same age as Felix, and I wasn't happy about old Simon Caspari's request until I met the boy. I'll admit I was charmed by him. Felix was a sturdy, handsome little fellow with chestnut curls and the nicest smile. He was also the opposite of my Sonny, an outgoing, confident, mischievous child. I gave Simon permission, and the two boys became playmates. Felix was always the leader, Sonny his faithful follower. Sonny was devoted to his little friend, and when the time came for him to go away to school, he was quite inconsolable. Felix, of course, attended a comprehensive. At sixteen Felix had had enough of school and begged me to send him to Paris to study cooking with a French chef." Mrs. Montrose gave a barking laugh. "Even at that age he had ideas far above his station in life."

"Felix had to settle for a dietitian course," Alice said indignantly. "He told me he felt Sybil had owed him more than that."

"I owed him *nothing*. But because of Sonny's attachment to the boy, I was generous enough to do that. When the course was finished, Felix took a job at a hospital in London and—"

"That's where I met him," Alice said dreamily. "I had a tonsillectomy and Felix came around to check my diet."

"And as soon as you were discharged from hospital, Felix moved into your flat and lived off you."

Alice glared at the older woman. "He hated that job and felt he was wasting his time at it. The pay was *terrible*."

"Mrs. Montrose," Miss Sanderson said. "Will you please continue."

"I will if Alice will allow me to. Where was I? Oh, yes. My son came down from Oxford and I was able to arrange a position for him at the Foreign Office. I was laying the groundwork for a career for Sonny. At the time I had high hopes for my son. He looked like his father, quite distinguished, and was well educated and beautifully mannered. All assets, and what he needed was a suitable wife. I started shopping around for the right girl. A wife with the proper background is so important, you see. At times I did despair of the boy. Sonny was so much like his father—dreamy, indecisive, rather weak. Then, rumors began to drift back to me. I checked and found he had resigned his position and was living with a—" It was Mrs. Montrose's turn to glare. "Alice, you'd better explain this part. After all, that girl was your friend."

"Blanche was never my friend." Alice turned her back to Mrs. Montrose and spoke directly to Miss Sanderson. "She was just a girl, much younger than me, who hung around the theater. When she wasn't there, she was on protest marches and sit-ins and things like that. Trying to save the world, you know. I didn't particularly like her, but I felt sorry for her. Blanche wasn't attractive and she seemed to have no friends or relatives. I took her in hand and gave her pointers on acting and her appearance." Alice preened. "I was quite pretty."

"She was." Mrs. Montrose gazed at the back of the mousy head. "An ash blond with a lovely skin and an excellent figure."

"Felix was always attracted by blondes—"

"I've noticed that," Mrs. Montrose remarked.

Without turning, Alice snapped, "Stop interrupting."

"Please," Miss Sanderson said wearily. "Alice, you said you introduced this girl to Sonny Montrose."

"I did. Sonny was still friendly with Felix, and they came around to the theater one evening. Blanche happened to be with me and I introduced Sonny to her." Alice looked past Miss Sanderson's shoulder. "It was like one of those love stories you read. Love at first sight. Both of them just speechless and thunderstruck." She giggled. "Felix thought it funny. Blanche was such a drab and Sonny a real stuffed shirt—"

"If you mean my son was a gentleman, you're quite correct."

Alice ignored this. "Blanche stopped coming to the the-

127

ater, and we heard Sonny had quit his job and moved in with her. I told Felix we really should tell Sybil, and he laughed and said she wouldn't hear about it from him. He said it served her right."

"About the reaction I would have expected from Felix." Patting her fluff of gray hair, the older woman continued, "When I did hear about my son, I went to London to get him out of that mess. The two of them were living in a dreadful loft over a garage, and when I saw it I was appalled. No real furniture, only a mattress on the floor and some cushions flung around. All the time I was there I was forced to stand. The girl was even worse than I'd feared. She was a common type for that era. What were they called? Flower children?"

"Hippies?" Miss Sanderson suggested.

"One of those unwashed creatures with hair dangling all over their faces. She was wearing a shapeless Indian print dress and had sandals on her grubby feet and strings of beads. She wore glasses, those odd ones—"

"Granny glasses." Alice added, "And she wasn't dirty. Blanche was always clean."

"When I saw my son I nearly had a stroke. Sonny had always been so immaculate, so well groomed. . . . He'd grown his hair long, started a beard, and was wearing a fringed jacket, sandals, strings of beads. Do you know what the boy was doing when I arrived?"

Perhaps smoking hashish through a hookah, Miss Sanderson thought.

The old woman said tragically, "He was strumming a *guitar*. Sonny told me he was writing protest songs. I talked until I was hoarse. Generally I could handle him with little effort, but he'd changed. . . . I couldn't sway him. Finally I appealed to the little tramp. I asked her if she wanted to ruin his life, told her if she truly loved my son she'd give him up. Sonny became furious and announced he'd found happiness and not only was he going to stay with the girl, but he intended to marry her. I can't even remember leaving them. I was completely shattered."

"What did you do?" Miss Sanderson asked.

"I went to Felix for help. He was shrewd and had influence with Sonny. Felix had been badgering me about funds to start a catering business, and I told him if he'd deliver my son back to me, I'd give him the money he wanted. As usual, Felix bargained and I agreed I'd also urge my friends to become his clients. I remember he laughed and said the price was right and he'd play the role of Judas— he'd break up the romance at once. All he wanted from me was to decoy Sonny down to our country home for a few days. I pretended I was ill and had our doctor summon my son to my side."

"And he came?"

"Yes. Sonny still had enough feeling for me to come." Leaning forward, Mrs. Montrose nudged Alice's back. "This is your first and only starring role. Tell Abigail all about it."

The widow didn't seem eager to begin. She fiddled with her wool, pulled down her skirt, tugged at the sleeve of her sweater. Miss Sanderson didn't prod, and at last the woman said huskily, "I suppose I should be ashamed, but Felix had his heart set on that catering business—"

"And he paid the price you demanded," Mrs. Montrose pointed out.

"Yes, he paid my price. He married me." Alice lifted beseeching eyes to Miss Sanderson. "Try to understand. We lived in my flat but . . . Felix always had other women. I didn't mind too much as long as he came back to me, but more than anything else I wanted the security of being his wife."

"I'm not here to judge," Miss Sanderson said crisply. "All I want are facts."

"It was so long ago anyway. Over twenty years and we were young and . . ." Alice straightened sagging shoulders. "At first Felix tried by himself. Women always went mad about him and he thought he could make Blanche fall for him and desert Sonny. So, as soon as Sonny returned home, Felix went to see Blanche. He turned on his charm and tried to seduce her. Much to his shock she threw him out of her loft. When he came back to our flat, he was furious. Then he calmed down and came up with another plan. For this one he needed my help. I'd heard him bargaining with Sybil and so I bargained with him. He gave me his word we'd be married."

"What did he need from you?" Miss Sanderson asked.

"Blanche wouldn't let Felix near her again, so he bought a bottle of her favorite wine and drugged it. I took it around to her loft, and at first she refused to let me in either. So I told her I'd come to apologize for Felix and then she did let me in. We sat on a couple of cushions and talked. I opened the wine and she drank a glass. The stuff worked quickly, and when she passed out, I unlocked the door and let Felix in. He carried her over to the mattress and undressed her. Then he stripped off his own clothes and got down with her. He made it look as though they were . . . well, you know. He'd brought the camera with him, and I took the pictures." With a touch of pride she added, "I'm awfully good at photography, and they were dandies. Clear as a bell. Felix had a friend develop them and then he gave the pictures to Sybil."

"There you are wrong," Mrs. Montrose said frigidly. "Felix didn't even bother showing them to me. He came down to our home, handed them to Sonny, and said something like, 'Take a good look at the little slut you want to marry.' Sonny looked at them and not a muscle in his face moved. Then he handed them back to Felix, got up, politely excused himself, and went to the library." She buried her face in her hands and her voice was muffled. "My son took his father's revolver and shot himself in the head. When we broke down the door, we found he was still alive. How I wish he'd finished the job properly!"

Miss Sanderson looked at the bowed head. "You buried him three weeks ago."

"I buried his shell." Her head jerked up. "You think me cold and unfeeling, worrying about a dinner party with my only child hardly in his grave. I suffered, Abigail, for years I suffered. but you must realize for twenty years my son was only marginally alive. His brain was so badly damaged that he never regained consciousness. Hooked up on a machine, tubes running in and out . . . When I finally won and he was allowed to die, I thanked God!"

"And you've always blamed Felix," Alice said bitterly. "Blamed Felix and me for doing what you wanted."

"I wanted my son back, alive and well, not as a living corpse. Yes, I blame you and Felix for what happened. Felix should have given those pictures to me, not to my son. I could have broken it gently to Sonny. He was such a sensitive boy, so much like his father."

Miss Sanderson was wondering how two such sensitive males could have borne a life with this woman. She asked, "What happened to the girl?"

The woman's simian face furrowed with displeasure. "She came storming into the hospital, demanding to see Sonny, making a horrible scene. She shouted she didn't believe me about his condition, that I was only trying to keep them apart. To quiet her I took her into his room, let her see him hooked up to that machine. I called in the specialist and asked him to explain Sonny's condition to her. Then she became quite calm. I told her to get out, never again to come near my son, never again to let me see her face. Before she left, she told me I was lucky he was still alive. She said, 'I'm certain, Mrs. Montrose, that we will meet again.' She quite upset me."

"The words don't sound threatening."

"Her voice was and so were her eyes. She had brown eyes, quite her nicest feature. Those eyes looked . . . inhuman. I must admit when I heard of her death a few years later, I felt relieved."

"She's dead?"

"I showed the article to Sybil." Alice had placidly resumed knitting and her needles flashed in the lamplight. "Only a short item on a back page. Blanche had gone to India with the Peace Corps or one of those things. She and another woman were taking a lorry loaded with medical supplies and food to a hill village when they had an accident. Some natives found them, took them to the nearest hospital, and Blanche died there."

"And how did you feel, Alice?" Miss Sanderson asked softly. "Relieved?"

"You *are* judging. I know it was a dirty thing to do, but to get Felix I would have killed."

Picking up the cat, Mrs. Montrose got to her feet. "Which you just did."

The younger woman leaped up and confronted her. "I know who the Jester is, Sybil. It's you! If I had been going to kill, I would have picked Dolly, not Felix!"

"Our Alice never did have any brains," Mrs. Montrose told the secretary. "Too bad she had to lose her looks. Well, any further questions?"

"Both of you sit down. I'm not finished. Do either of you know the names of the family involved in the accident that killed Damien Day?"

Mrs. Montrose shook her head. "I paid little attention to it at the time."

"Alice, you showed Reggie a letter from the child's father. Surely you remember."

132

"The child's name was Bonny. Yes, Bonny Wilson. I don't remember the mother's name. The father . . . I saw his name on the check he returned to Felix." Alice's low brow crinkled. "It began with a *C*."

"Charles, Calvin, Clifford?"

"No, something uncommon. I can't recall what it was. Why?"

Disregarding the question, Miss Sanderson asked, "What did Blanche look like?"

"I told you," Mrs. Montrose said impatiently. "Like a hippy. Except for her eyes, I don't remember anything but those awful clothes."

"Alice?"

"It's all so hazy. She was about your height, very thin, long straight brown hair. I can't even remember her features."

"Is there anything else either of you can think of?"

"One thing," Mrs. Montrose said with relish. "It probably is of no importance, but our hostess was once Felix's mistress. While they were both working on that cooking show. Alice, don't look at me like that. You know it as well as I do. Felix told me about it. Told me a joke about doing his interviews on the casting couch."

"Nancy?" Miss Sanderson was sitting bolt upright.

"Nancy Canard as she was then. Felix always had a weakness for pretty blondes."

"Does Gavin know?"

"I've no idea. And I've no further information."

"You can both go," Miss Sanderson said abruptly. "Ask Nancy and Gavin to step in."

"Both of them?"

"You heard me."

Mrs. Montrose picked up Omar. "No need to snap my head off," she said, and swept from the room. Alice, beginning to weep again, stumbled along in her wake.

133

Miss Sanderson was glad to see them go. That matriarch had enjoyed telling her about Nancy and Felix. Getting up, she paced around the saloon bar. She noticed that yet another of Noel Canard's paintings hung on the far wall. She refused to look closely at it.

The door from the public bar swung open, and the Lebonhoms entered. Miss Sanderson's eyes wandered past Nancy and settled on the man behind her.

CHAPTER ELEVEN

Both husband and wife appeared to be in better spirits. In fact, Gavin was more relaxed than Miss Sanderson had yet seen him, and Nancy had regained her fresh color. Gavin selected the chair at the far end of the table, and Nancy pulled the footstool over and slumped down beside him, one elbow braced on his gray-flanneled knee. He looked earnestly down the table at Miss Sanderson. "I've given this some thought. . . ."

Lord, she thought, now we work through another plot of a mystery he has read or perhaps has written. "I've come to two conclusions," he continued. "There's no possible reason why the murderer—the Jester, as you've dubbed him—can wish to harm me. And there's no chance either you or the police can suspect me of having killed Felix. As you explained, the Jester was used to play a rotten trick on *me*." He gave a booming laugh. "Can you picture my helping to ruin my play?"

"You and Nancy told me about Felix's peculiar sense of humor. Perhaps it was perverse enough to enjoy forcing you to help him make you a laughingstock."

Gavin laughed again. "What a wild imagination you have! How could he possibly have done that?"

Not having that answer, Miss Sanderson turned to the young woman. "Nancy, I understand you and Felix were once . . . more than friends."

"Mrs. Montrose and Alice have been gossiping, I see."

The older woman's eyes wandered back to Gavin. He was placidly and rather messily charging a pipe. Dark grains of tobacco spilled down his shirt and littered the tabletop. "If you'd rather speak alone . . ."

"It's no secret, Auntie Abby, and Gavin knows all about it. For a few months Felix and I were lovers." Leaning forward, the girl confided, "My analyst tells me I'm attracted to older men because of my childhood. Seeking a father image, you know. And he's right. Since I was a child, older men have always attracted me, acted almost like a magnet. My first affair was with a history teacher. I was only fourteen at the time and he was—"

"For God's sake, Nan, Abigail didn't ask the story of your life!"

Miss Sanderson tapped her pen against the table. "Then Felix didn't force you into this . . . ah, intimate relationship?"

"Of course not! When Felix showed interest in me, I was delighted. He was so attractive and so good in bed."

Involuntarily, Miss Sanderson again looked at Gavin. He was now lighting his pipe. "Who broke this affair off?"

"Felix." She pouted. "As soon as the show finished, he lost interest in me that way. But we stayed friends. Don't look so stern. The world is much different now than when you and mother were girls."

"Chuck full of liberated women," Gavin agreed. "All living their lives as they please."

Wonderful new world, Miss Sanderson thought. And when Felix Caspari had been born out of wedlock, his mother had been branded a loose woman for doing exactly what these liberated women prided themselves on. She took a deep breath. "Gavin, were you aware of Nancy's relationship with Felix at the time of your marriage?"

"Not only that affair, but all her others. All with older men, of course. Shortly before we were married, Nan managed to keep me awake for hours confessing all. After the first couple of exposés I did doze off. Rather boring, like being forced to watch reruns on television."

His wife was now pouting charmingly. "Don't be beastly, darling."

"How old are you, Gavin?"

"I fail to see what that has to do with a murder." Apparently women weren't the only ones sensitive about their ages. Gavin reddened slightly and puffed out a cloud of aromatic smoke. Finally he grunted, "Old enough to be Nancy's father."

"I suppose," the girl said dreamily, "that's why I shamelessly threw myself at him when we met at a party. But you wouldn't be interested in that."

"I'm interested."

"It was shortly after mother's funeral. I was feeling so depressed that I decided I must cheer myself up, and I went to a party a friend was throwing. Allison was a makeup girl, and we'd become friendly while we were both working on the cooking show. It was a hectic affair, rock music booming and people shouting to make themselves heard above it. Really a crush too, Allison's flat is so tiny. I was sorry I went and then I spotted Gavin. He was so yummy I simply followed around after him but"—she turned and looked up at her husband—"he completely ignored me."

"I did notice her, Abigail. She was so pretty but so young. I steered clear of her."

"Not for long you didn't." His young wife smiled complacently. "When Gavin went to the drink table, I tagged along behind him. Allison came over to chat and she was teasing me about this inn. Asked what I planned to do with my white elephant. I told her the only possible thing I could do was sell the island and the Jester. Let someone else worry about the damn place. Then Allison asked about Felix, and I told her we'd broken up but were still good friends. Suddenly Gavin stopped ignoring me and he took me home and—"

"Nancy promptly took me to bed."

"I thought with Gavin it was only a passing fancy. But lo and behold, he asked me to marry him. In fact"—she looked around the saloon bar—"he proposed in this room. We'd come down for a weekend and he fell in love with this inn." She waved smoke away from her face. "I often tease him about falling in love with the inn, not with me."

Her husband made no effort to deny this, and Miss Sanderson flipped to a clean page. I feel ancient, she thought, quite out of tune. "Tell me how Felix Caspari came to be funding your renovations."

"It was Gavin's idea," Nancy said firmly.

"You're upsetting your Auntie Abby." Gavin chuckled. "She's struggling with the concept of a bridegroom borrowing money from his wife's ex-lover. But any port in a storm, and Felix was the only person I could touch for a loan. I'd made the rounds of the banks and so on, but the only collateral we had was this island and the inn, and they refused to lend a pound on them. So, I had Nancy invite Felix down here, and he saw the potential for turning this place into a fashionable murder-party house. I explained I'd be writing the scripts myself, and he became wildly enthusiastic. Felix put up what seemed to be an enormous amount of cash, and we had legal papers drawn up and then got to work."

"And you and Felix got along amicably?"

Nancy giggled. "At first. Gavin was kowtowing to Felix, yes sir, no sir, anything you say, sir. Then the money started to run out and it became a bit dicey."

"That was Felix's fault," Gavin said hotly. "Insisted on having that suite done over with the latest decorating and expensive furnishings. I told him it doesn't fit in with the rest of the inn and cost too much, but he had to have his way. Do you realize, Abigail, that with the money spent there I could have installed central heating and electricity?"

"Now who's getting off the track?" his wife asked.

Miss Sanderson said patiently, "Whose idea was this party?"

"Felix's," Gavin grated. "Another of his damn fool notions. I tried to get him to hold off, wait until we either got this place finished or have the first party in the spring. But no, the great man had spoken."

Nancy placed a chubby hand on his knee. "Don't rave on, darling. Felix was very good about it. Provided all the food, most of the booze, and arranged for the guests. How could you ever have gotten Dolores Carter-White, Mrs. Montrose, and the Black Knight down here?"

"I couldn't have," he admitted. "After I thought it over, it did sound like a wonderful chance for publicity."

Miss Sanderson dug out her cigarette pack and lighter. "Who suggested Robby as a guest?"

"Felix," Nancy told her. "I told him about you and Mother being such chums when you were girls, and he was excited. He said Reggie Knight wanted to meet Robert Forsythe and ordered me to go to London, see you, and make sure your employer came to the party. I failed, of course, and when I told Felix and Gavin, they were both furious. Felix said he knew Reggie would beg off if he knew Mr. Forsythe wouldn't be here, and also that Mrs. Montrose was frantic to meet him too. Finally Felix cooled down and swore us to secrecy. No one else knew about you, Auntie Abby."

"I noticed that," Miss Sanderson said wryly. She added silently, And I devotedly wish Robby were right here instead of me. "Tell me, Gavin, what was the board meeting about in Felix's suite last night."

Gavin had been knocking the dottle from his pipe. At her question he hit the glass ashtray so hard it bounced. "The absolute heartless bastard!"

His wife clutched his arm. "Let me explain, darling. You get so violent." The round face turned to Miss Sanderson. "This is one time I agree with Gavin. Felix took us up there, gave us a drink of his ruddy brandy, and told us he was in immediate need of money. The legal papers we'd signed entitled him to demand his money whenever he wished. Felix said we had to raise that money, and if we didn't, he'd foreclose and sell the inn."

Miss Sanderson was frowning. "I should have thought Felix made a great deal of money."

"He did," Gavin said bitterly. "And he spent money like water. On women and gambling and his lifestyle. Felix told Nan and me that he was stony and had to settle gambling debts and raise the funds to get rid of Alice and marry Dolly. I tried my best to reason with him, suggested he might borrow from Mrs. Montrose. Felix admitted there was a chance for a loan if he could persuade Dolly to attend the woman's bloody dinner party; he said Mrs. Montrose had hinted at it. But then he told us that Dolly was stubborn and he didn't think she'd agree. So . . . we left it at that. I could have *killed* him!"

Spinning around, Nancy stared up at him. Gavin patted her shoulder and gave a shaky laugh. "Of course, I didn't. Simply an expression all of us use. And Abigail, what I said earlier still goes. Felix would never have picked me as a confederate to play a lousy joke on myself."

Her cool eyes examined him. "What if he had offered to hold off on the foreclosure of the Jester for the price of your help."

"Ridiculous!"

But his wife was nodding. "Oddly enough, it sounds like the diabolic way Felix's mind worked. He might have been pretending to be broke just to force Gavin to—"

"Nan! What a lovely little helpmate you are."

"And what a sickening excuse for a husband you are!" Nancy burst into tears. "All you ever wanted was this horrible inn. I hope you do lose it."

"If I do, my child bride, you can get lost too!"

Nancy was sobbing, and her husband's hands had tightened into fists. Miss Sanderson snapped, "If you want to continue your family fight, go elsewhere. If not, let's get on with it."

Gavin sighed. "We'd better get this done. Nan, stop sniveling. You know I don't mean half what I say. I've been under a strain and so have you." He pulled out a handkerchief and handed it to her. "Next question, Abigail?"

"Tell me about your background."

"That I can do in one sentence. I want to be a writer, I've always wanted to be a writer, and I'm damned well going to be a writer."

"In the meantime you had to support yourself. Or did you inherit an income?"

"Hardly. All I inherited was a few sticks of furniture from a father who was a postal clerk. I've had so many jobs I can't remember all of them. Clerked in shops, tried to sell insurance, at one time worked for an estate agent. Earned barely enough to survive, but all I was interested in was writing."

"Was this your first marriage?"

"Second. Ann and I were divorced years ago."

"Any children?"

"One who died young. I suppose that's why my marriage broke up. After our child's death my wife was never the same."

141

Nancy was gazing soulfully up at him. "I never knew that."

"It wouldn't have interested you. Too involved with your own affairs, romantic or otherwise."

"That's a *beastly* thing to say. You—"

"That's enough, Nancy," Miss Sanderson said. "Among your numerous jobs, Gavin, did you ever act?"

"Not professionally. Ann and I were members of a drama society for a time. For amateurs we weren't bad and put on some fair shows. Why?"

"Only wondered." Miss Sanderson closed her notebook. "That covers it."

Gavin rose and his wife, wiping at damp eyes, got up too. Gavin asked brightly, "Any of the interviews thus far shed any light on Felix's death?"

"All of them. Four people—four motives."

He brushed at his mustache. "Doesn't take a detective to see Alice Caspari's. But what about Sybil Montrose?"

"Confidential information."

Nancy said rather shrewdly, "It might be connected with her son. Felix mentioned they were close friends. But what about Gavin and me?"

Gavin draped a long arm around his wife's shoulders. "Abigail is toying with the idea that I could have killed Felix to keep him from taking this inn away from me."

"Auntie Abby, that's *silly*. Felix's estate will be inherited by Alice. She'll probably do the same thing."

Her husband explained, "Felix's death does let me off the hook for a time. Perhaps give me a chance to come up with the money. And perhaps Alice will be more amenable than Felix would have been."

"Precisely," Miss Sanderson said.

"But what about me?" Nancy asked. "I certainly

wouldn't kill Felix or anyone else just to keep this awful inn."

Her husband chuckled. "Woman scorned. Right, Abigail?"

"Right. Felix won your affection, Nancy, discarded you, and then turned up for your party not only with his wife but with the woman he intended to marry."

"That is nonsense!" Nancy's eyes blazed. "Come up to date. Women aren't like that anymore."

"My child, emotions don't change that much. Even in your brave new world, love and jealousy and hate still exist."

"You're horrible! So cold and not at all as I thought you'd be. I pictured you exactly like my mother. Gentle and kind."

Miss Sanderson rose and looked down at the vividly angry face. Rather sadly she said, "We were both disappointed. I had pictured you exactly as your mother was."

The girl bristled and Gavin pulled at her arm. "Come now," he muttered.

The door leading to the kitchen banged open and Reggie called, "Soup's on. Come and get it."

Spinning on her heels, Nancy stalked out of the saloon bar. Her husband followed, and as he passed the other man he said, "Women!"

Miss Sanderson's shoulders sagged and she rubbed at her brow. Reggie asked, "Little trouble?"

"Two worlds colliding. You go along. I'm not hungry."

"Seems to me you were the one mentioning keeping up our strength." He added, "You are eating if I have to—"

"My head is pounding and—" She smashed a fist down on the notebook. "It's no good. I can't be a detective. All I'm fit for is taking notes and asking stupid questions."

He put a consoling arm around her shoulders. "A couple

of aspirin and some hot chow and you'll feel better. Abigail, you have no choice. The Jester isn't keeping us here to play parlor games with us. And you're the only one who can—"

"I know." She lifted her chin. "Lead on to that chow."

CHAPTER TWELVE

THE KITCHEN PROVED TO BE UNEXPECTEDLY CHEERFUL. The long table had been covered with a gay tartan cloth, and extra lamps had been brought in. Miss Sanderson, with aspirin provided by Fran and a heaping plate of shepherd's pie and vegetable salad dished up by Reggie, was soon feeling more cheerful. Her companions chatted determinedly, but by tacit agreement no mention was made of murder or Felix Caspari. Mrs. Montrose was exerting her considerable charm on Dolly Carter-White, and their host was being as charming to, and most solicitous of, the widow. Alice apparently was taking her new status seriously and had changed from her shapeless skirt and sweater to a shapeless black dress. Nancy Lebonhom bent her head over her plate, assiduously keeping her swollen eyes away from Miss Sanderson. Hielkje, despite her ill health, managed to tuck a copious supper away.

The first to leave the table was the Widow Caspari. Gavin jumped up to pull her chair back and murmured something in her ear. Alice said somberly, "Thank you, but no. I'd prefer to be alone." She looked around the table. "I suppose you people think I'm putting on an act. I know at times Felix could be . . . he did humiliate me and treat me badly, but . . . I wouldn't have stayed with him all those years if that was the way he treated me all the time. He didn't. Felix was often kind and thoughtful. I'm going to sit in the alcove and remember those times." She picked up her knitting bag. "This will soothe my nerves."

"We understand," Gavin said earnestly. "I'd better build that fire up so you'll be warm and—"

"No. You're kind, Gavin, but I'll do it. So many things to remember . . ."

On that trailing sorrowful note she made a stately exit. Conversation faltered and died. One by one the others drifted out of the kitchen until only the cook and Dolly were left with Miss Sanderson. Pulling her heavy body up, Hielkje started to clear the table. Then she thumped a stack of plates down and muttered, "Forgot completely about my medication." She sighed. "Have to go all the way up those stairs for it."

The baize door swung to behind her, and Dolly sat silently for a time. Then she reached for a plate of fruit and cheese and told Miss Sanderson, "I suppose it's my turn to be grilled. Let's do it here. Much warmer than in the saloon bar."

Miss Sanderson selected a piece of Brie. "Would you tell me about your background. Your family and so on."

"Family? I don't remember my father. He was a construction worker and was killed on the job shortly before my second birthday. When I was about eight, Momma remarried. My stepfather and I never got along. He was a nasty, miserable little man, obviously resentful of the child who had been foisted on him. Momma died of pneumonia when I was sixteen, and my stepfather made it clear I was no longer welcome in his house, so I struck off on my own."

Her eyes intent on the pear she was peeling, Dolly continued, "For nine years I held an assortment of jobs.

Clerked in dress shops and bookshops and for a short and grim time, in a cardboard-box factory. When I was twenty-five my stepfather died suddenly—heart attack. Rather surprised me. I'd never associated an organ like that with him." She raised brilliant emerald eyes. "Then I had another surprise. He'd left a legacy for me. Not a fortune, but sufficient to do what I'd always wanted. I rented the cottage on the moors and wrote my first book. As I told you, my agent, Rory, entered my life and Dolores Carter-White was born. And she has lived happily for the past twelve years. I suppose you'll want to hear about Felix?"

"Please."

Hielkje, who had quietly returned, dropped a pot and swore, but Miss Sanderson didn't look away from the woman opposite her. "You met Felix in Italy," she prompted.

"At a restaurant in Venice. I'd just finished a book and was exhausted. I was also irritable, and when I couldn't find the dish I wanted on the menu, I became quite curt with my waiter. I'd noticed Felix with a group of people at the next table, and I'd recognized him immediately. From his TV show and cookbooks, you know."

"Did he recognize you too?"

"From the way he was staring, I'd say yes. He heard me complaining to the waiter and came over to my table and told the poor man that if this lovely lady had her heart set on *ris de veau,* she must have it. I protested, but Felix said the chef wouldn't mind and made straight for the kitchen." Tinted lips parted over the perfect teeth. "From the roars issuing from that kitchen I assumed the other chef deeply resented Felix's invasion. Then Felix was back, bowing and kissing my hand, and put down the best dish of *ris de veau* I had ever tasted. He ordered champagne, and of course I had to ask him to have a glass. One thing led to another, and Felix escorted me to my hotel." The smile

147

widened and became a laugh. "He had every desire to escort me into bed, but that was too high a price even for that dish. He took my rejection as a challenge and from then on was my shadow, showering me with invitations, flowers, gifts."

Hielkje had given up any effort at work and was staring at the author. "And you fell in love," she murmured.

The blond head turned and Dolly laughed again. "Been reading my books, Hielkje? Sorry, no romance in this story." She turned back to Miss Sanderson. "Felix really wasn't capable of love, but he was terribly obsessed and infatuated. As for me . . . frankly, I felt it time to marry and he seemed suitable husband material."

"Despite the small fact he was already married," Miss Sanderson said dryly.

An elegant shoulder moved in a tiny shrug. "According to Felix, merely a marriage of convenience. One he kept on with only because he'd never found a woman he wanted enough to bother divorcing for."

"You felt no pity for Alice Caspari?"

"Not a whit. She's such a doormat. The only time Alice showed any spirit was when she downed jenever, and that was only bottle courage. But Alice shouldn't have worried. By the time we arrived for this so-called party, I was having second thoughts."

Miss Sanderson lifted a bunch of green grapes onto her plate. This then was the author of her favorite books. Warm, passionate tales of love and sacrifice, of man and woman working through all the obstacles one could imagine to find happiness ever after. Dolly must have been following her thoughts. She said lightly, "I think I've disillusioned you, Abigail. But I only write the plots, I don't live them. Where was I?"

"Having second thoughts about your not-so-true love."

A wrinkle appeared between the startling eyes. "At first

Felix seemed ideal. He was handsome, physically appealing, a public figure. He seemed an asset, but I soon found he had faults. He was a spendthrift, carelessly tossing money around. I didn't care for that. I value money. And that sense of humor of his! It was cruel, at times verging on sadistic."

Miss Sanderson pulled off a grape, then put it down on her plate. "Did he tell you about the joke he was planning to pull on Gavin?"

"Not a word. But then, he knew well how I felt about his jokes."

"I take it you aren't mourning him?"

"I feel badly about his death, yes. But his widow is doing enough mourning for both of us." She rose gracefully. "Any further questions?"

"One. Have you ever done any acting?"

"No." Dolly smiled down at the older woman. "But writers are supposedly closely allied to actors."

As Dolly left, Miss Sanderson followed her with her cool gaze. And are you an actress? she asked silently. Could it have been Felix Caspari who was having second thoughts?

Hielkje bustled over and started stacking plates. "She isn't a bit like I thought she'd be," the cook confided. "But none of these celebrities are. Mrs. Montrose isn't even polite, and Reggie is much nicer than I thought a rock star would be."

"And Felix Caspari?"

"He was a *sjoelke*." Hielkje paused and then added piously, "But he is dead and may his soul rest in peace and go to *Himmel*." She gestured at the mounds of dishes, cutlery, and pots. "So much to do all by myself. It will take a long time before I finish up and you can interview me."

Taking the hint, Miss Sanderson rose. "I'll give you a hand and we can talk while we work."

When she reached the sink, she found she was the one faced with the washing up, while Hielkje, clutching a dish towel, waited. Rolling up her sleeves, Miss Sanderson plunged her hands into the hot soapy water. Hielkje was able to talk faster than she worked and a gush of words flowed from her. Patiently, Miss Sanderson washed dishes and separated the wheat from the chaff. Father Visser had been Frisian and his wife English. Their only child, Hielkje, had been born in Leeuwarden, and shortly after the child's birth Mrs. Visser and her daughter had deserted father Visser and returned to England and a stern Chapel family.

"I was never told why we left my father," Hielkje confided. "Mother simply called him 'that rotter,' and she didn't care much for me either, always said I looked just like 'that rotter.' The only times she was decent to me was when I was sick. As soon as I could, I left home and went to London to look for work."

Miss Sanderson rinsed the last dish and started on the cutlery. It appeared that Hielkje had had as many jobs as Dolly and Gavin had had. Her health was "not robust" and her employers too demanding. She was close to thirty before she had her first suitor and seized the opportunity to marry and retire to a life of ease. It hadn't quite worked out that way. "Eric had a farm in Kenya," Hielkje explained. "I thought it would be a good life with oodles of servants, but when I got there, I found all he'd been looking for was unpaid labor. Eric turned out to be a slave driver." Her brown eyes indignant, she recalled those days. "I've always had a heavy build and look strong, but my health is poor and I simply couldn't stand it. Finally I appealed to my mother, and she did send me my return fare, but she told me I'd made my own bed and when I came back would have to make my own living. So I drifted from job to job, and then I spotted Peggy Canard's advertisement and came down here to apply."

Miss Sanderson was doggedly scouring a pan. From then on, she thought, Hielkje had had an easy life, an understanding employer in Peggy and with Fran to do most of the work. "And you've been happy here, Hielkje?"

"It's been the best part of my life. Peggy was wonderful to me and Fran . . . Fran's been like a mother. In fact, much more motherly than my own ever was."

The secretary lifted her head and gazed at the other woman. Hielkje looked years older than Fran Hornblower. She put her thoughts into words. "You're younger than Fran?"

"Only a few months younger. I know I look older than my age, but that's because of my health, you see. Poor health ages one dreadfully. Yes, we were all very content until Felix Caspari came down and started to boss us around."

"Did Felix ever bring his wife with him when the inn was being renovated?"

"He always came alone. Neither Fran nor I liked the man. Always ordering us around and complaining. But he could be thoughtful. Felix brought me Dutch chocolate a couple of times and bought that pea jacket for Fran. All she had was a thin jacket, and he said she needed something warmer. Strange man." Draping the towel over a rod, Hielkje stretched. "Thank goodness that's done." She sank on a chair and watched her companion scrubbing out the sink. "Many hands make light work, Abigail."

Miss Sanderson rolled down her sleeves and picked up the notebook and the bag of keys. "Shall we turn off the lamps?"

"Better leave them. Fran is probably gathering up the others to clean and fill."

After the warmth of the kitchen the hall seemed even

151

colder than usual. Shivering, Miss Sanderson picked up a flashlight, wondering if she'd ever be truly warm again. Then she cocked her head and asked Hielkje, "Did you hear anything?"

"Only the wind." Hielkje yawned. "Well, I'm off. Good night."

Miss Sanderson paused at the door leading to the guest wing and then changed her mind and wandered down the hall to the lobby. The door of the dining room opened and Fran pushed one of the metal wagons out. "No rest for the wicked," she told Miss Sanderson. "You look exhausted. Should be in bed."

"That's where I was going when I heard some kind of thud. Did you drop something?"

Fran pointed at the wagon. Both shelves held rows of lamps. "Nary a one. Must have been a shutter banging. I'll gather up the lamps in the public bar and that should do it."

Miss Sanderson held open a door, and Fran pushed the wagon into the bar. She stopped abruptly. The secretary peered over her shoulder. Then they both knelt beside a figure crumpled near the counter. "Nancy," Miss Sanderson moaned. "Fran, is she . . ."

"She's fainted. Get a couple of cushions from the alcove and I'll prop her feet up." Fran lifted her head and her nostrils quivered. "Do you smell something burning?"

"Smells like cloth." Pulling herself up, Miss Sanderson headed toward the alcove. As she reached the narrow passage between the benches, she could see the source of the smell. A ball of purple wool, badly scorched, rested on the hearth rug. Miss Sanderson's eyes traveled from the wool to a foot shod in a heavy black brogue and then followed the leg up to the hem of a black dress. Stepping into the alcove, she stood over the figure huddled on the bench, the mousy head turned toward the dying fire. Alice Caspari, looking deep in sleep. Miss Sanderson put out a hand and touched a shoulder. The head sagged forward, and from an ear something long and thin and shiny stuck out like an obscene antenna.

"Abigail," Fran called. "Be quick with those cushions."

Gulping, Miss Sanderson backed away from the hearth. "I think," she said unsteadily, "you'd better come here." Dimly she was aware of Fran beside her, of the ponytail of brown hair falling over the shoulder of the pea jacket.

"Get yourself a drink," Fran ordered. "Can't have you passing out too."

Miss Sanderson found herself behind the counter, a glass clutched in one hand, a bottle of Glenfiddich in the other. Funny, she had no memory of reaching for the bottle or glass. Then Fran was on the other side of the counter. "You'll have to see to Nancy. I'm going to get . . . I guess it better be Reggie. Gavin is useless."

When Fran returned with the singer, Miss Sanderson was seated on the floor, Nancy's head in her lap. Nancy was moaning, rolling her head from side to side. Reggie looked down at her. "Is she all right?"

"She will be." Miss Sanderson's voice had steadied. She held the glass to the girl's pale lips and Nancy's teeth chattered against its rim. "I'd better get her up to her room."

That was easier said than done. Most of the girl's weight sagged against the secretary's thin body. At the top of the staircase she let the girl sag to the floor, ran down the hall, and banged on the study door. From the other side of that door a voice quavered, "Who is it?"

"Abigail. Get out here and look after your wife."

Without waiting for the door to be unlocked she sped back down the hall to Nancy. Gavin joined them, and he seemed more annoyed than anxious. "What in hell is wrong with her now? Did she see another ghost?"

153

"She saw Alice Caspari with a knitting needle driven into an ear," Miss Sanderson said brutally.

Gavin Lebonhom collapsed beside his wife. He grasped at his thick hair as though about to wrench it out by the roots. "This is a *nightmare*. I keep hoping I'll wake up and—"

"Wake up and look after Nancy," Miss Sanderson snapped, and raced down the stairs.

When she panted into the public bar, she found Fran and Reggie perched on stools, gulping Glenfiddich. Reggie was wearing striped pajamas, a heavy robe, and sheepskin slippers. Taking the bottle, Miss Sanderson poured a hefty drink. She told her companions, "This time we know exactly how long the Jester had. From the time supper was finished until Nancy came in here. She must have come for a drink. This bottle and a glass were on the counter."

Fran nodded. "Probably smelled burning wool as we did and went over to fish the ball from the coals. She must have thought Alice was asleep, and then she saw that needle—"

"Ran to get help and fainted." Miss Sanderson propped her back against the counter. "Tha must have been the thud I heard." Leaning around Reggie, she asked Fran, "Would it be difficult to kill a person like that?"

"Easy and fast." Picking up a swizzle stick, Fran grabbed Reggie's chin with her free hand and pushed the stick into his ear.

He wrenched away. "Find another model. What do we do now?"

"Cope," Miss Sanderson said morosely. "Do the best we can until this bloody storm dies down and we can get help."

"What will we do about . . ." He pointed at the alcove.

"We certainly can't leave her there," Fran said. "We'd

154

better put her on the dumbwaiter and take her up to the attic."

The nightmare that Gavin had mentioned came alive in the next hour. Armed with flashlights and lamps, the three went up to the attic where the pathetic remains of Alice Caspari rested on the platform of the dumbwaiter. Mercifully she was lighter and limper than her husband had been, and Reggie was able to lift her unaided onto the door that Fran and Miss Sanderson brought from the boxroom. The eyes of the mannequins glittered eerily as the door was lowered and a rose velvet curtain draped over the small figure in the black mourning dress. Motes of dust billowed up from the curtain and lamplight danced against the walls.

Fran looked down at the two doors and their dreadful burdens and scrubbed her palms down her jeans. "The Jester had better call a halt. We're running out of doors and old curtains." She began to laugh, a shrill and ragged sound that alerted Reggie and Miss Sanderson.

Putting a comforting arm around the woman's shoulders, he guided her from the room, and by the time they reached the bottom of the ladderlike stairs, Fran's laughter had dissolved into tears. As they moved past Gavin's study, the door creaked open and he peered through the crack. "Everything under control?" he whispered.

"Just ducky." Fran began to laugh again. "Instead of building on another guest wing, you'd better enlarge the attic. It's cold enough for a mortuary but not big—"

"For God's sake," he snapped. "You're acting as neurotic as Nan is."

"You must excuse us poor females," she said shrilly. "Cracking up just from finding and disposing of bodies."

Gavin snarled, "Snap out of it—"

"You'd better get that door shut," Reggie told him evenly. "One more asinine word and I'll knock you down."

The door slammed so hard it rocked on its hinges. Pulling herself away from Reggie, Fran wiped the sleeve of her jacket over her eyes. "Tantrum all over, folks. Sorry about that."

"Don't be," Miss Sanderson told her warmly. "You're a tower of strength, but even crusaders have limits. Can I give you a hand getting to bed?"

Fran managed a smile. "Not that far gone yet, Abigail. Anyway, I have to get those lamps cleaned up."

Taking her shoulders, Reggie steered her down the hall toward her room. "Not to worry. This knight will attend to the night lights. And no, Abigail, I never did a stint in a lamp factory, but we used them a number of times in Liverpool when my parents neglected to pay the electric bill."

As Fran stepped into her room, Miss Sanderson told him, "You're a man of many talents, Reggie Knight."

He waved toward Fran's door. "And that's one wonderful lady." He smiled down at Miss Sanderson. "And you're another one."

"Flattery will get your everything. I'll give you a hand."

They retrieved the wagon loaded with lamps from the public bar and took it to the kitchen. They worked quickly with Miss Sanderson wiping the globes and her companion trimming the wicks and filling the bowls. As Reggie put the last one on the table, he asked, "Care to talk or too tired?"

"I don't feel tired at all. Strange. Earlier I was reeling with fatigue. Now I feel quite keyed up."

"Adrenaline flowing. My room or yours?"

"Mine."

He opened the door of the guest wing. "I'd better stop off and get my flask."

"I have supplies of my own." She opened the door of her room. "You stir the fire up and I'll pour."

156

He picked up a coal scuttle. "Wonder how brandy will sit on top of Glenfiddich?"

"We'll soon know."

He raised his glass. "Cheers." Then he gave her a wry grin. "Are you thinking you may be drinking with a murderer?"

"The thought has occurred to me." Leaning forward, she touched her glass to his. "Here's to good hunting."

CHAPTER THIRTEEN

Sᴉɴᴋɪɴɢ ᴛᴏ ᴀ ᴄʜᴀɪʀ, Rᴇɢɢɪᴇ ᴛᴜʀɴᴇᴅ ᴀɴ ᴜɴsᴍɪʟɪɴɢ face on her. "You're taking one hell of a chance. It would be simple for me to finish you off and none the wiser."

"Using what for a weapon?"

He glanced around. "The Jester seems to use anything handy. Felix's knife, Alice's knitting needle. Now, down to cases. Allow me to read your mind, Sherlock. After our conversation about Damien's death you think I may have despaired of meting out punishment to Felix by legal means and decided to give it to him myself.

"It's possible."

"Poor Alice had nothing to do with my brother. Why would I kill her?"

"To cover up the first murder. Felix could have let slip to his wife the name of the person who was going to help him play the trick with the dumbwaiter."

"Explain this. When you were describing the way her husband was killed, why didn't Alice spring to her feet and point an accusing finger at me?"

Miss Sanderson gazed into the flames. "She didn't strike me as an intelligent woman. Felix may only have hinted at the identity of his confederate and she wasn't certain it was you. But later Alice could have come up with the answer, perhaps mentioned something that alerted you and—"

"And I followed her to the public bar and rammed a knitting needle into her dull little brain." He pushed back a ringlet. "I'm about to blow your theory into smithereens. Alice would have had to alert me *after* Felix's murder. Right?" Miss Sanderson nodded, and he asked, "Then why did I sneak out and put the boat out of commission the night *before* Felix was killed?"

"You wouldn't have had the slightest reason to do that. And that's why we're here alone. Do you think I'd have been foolish enough to be alone with you if I'd thought you are the Jester? As a matter of fact you are the one person in this inn I feel I can trust."

He held out his glass. "Let's have a drink on it. Much more of this and I may switch from beer to spirits. Abigail, my offer to be your Watson still holds. Want to bounce ideas off?"

She jumped up and started to pace. "Can you recall the names of the family members who were involved in your brother's accident?"

"Those names are practically engraved on my mind. Wilson—mother Jean, daughter Bonny, father Cuthbert."

"Did you ever see Cuthbert Wilson? Even a picture of him?"

He shook his head. "Only picture I saw was in a newspaper, and that was only of Jean and her daughter. Pretty blurry at that. You're toying with the idea that Wilson is the Jester. But there's nobody in this place who suits the bill. Except..."

"Yes," she said. "Except a man who seems a quivering mass of fear. A man who admitted he once appeared in amateur theatrics. A man who also admitted he had once been married, his child is dead, and his wife 'never was the same after the child's death.'"

"Gavin Lebonhom! No, that's too much of a coincidence. Being right here on the spot when Felix . . . Abigail, I don't believe in coincidences."

"Neither do I. Try this out. Gavin met Nancy at a party. He showed no interest in her until he overheard one of her conversations. Nancy has a suspicion that the mention of this inn was the reason for his sudden attention. But the woman she was talking to had also talked about Felix Caspari and her relationship with him."

"Got you again, Holmes! Felix was back and forth to this place any number of times this year. Seems to me if Gavin was Wilson, he had ample opportunity to avenge his family long before now."

"Numbers."

"Huh?"

"Normally there are only four people here. Gavin, Nancy, Fran, and Hielkje. Right at present we have four more people to cloud the issue."

"Again, Gavin had no reason to harm poor Alice. Oh . . . same reason you gave for me. Felix let drop a hint about his helper. . . . No, it won't wash. Why maroon us all if Gavin had got his target?"

Miss Sanderson made a swift turn and dropped back into her chair. "I might be able to answer that if I could figure some way Gavin could get off this island."

"Make his escape, you mean?"

"Right. Let's face it, Reggie, all we have to go on is what these people have told us. Any of them could be lying through his or her teeth. But the police . . . Lord! How I wish I had their facilities. They can dig into backgrounds and find out in a short time whether Gavin Lebonhom and Cuthbert Wilson are one and the same. If Gavin is the Jester, his only hope is to run for it."

"I take your point." He rubbed his jaw. "But the only way I can see to get off this island is either by the causeway, and that certainly can't be used until this storm dies down, or by flying." He lifted his dark eyes. "You think any one of the others might be the Jester? What about Nancy Lebonhom?"

Tersely she explained what she had learned about Nancy and her affair with Felix. His teeth flashed whitely and he said, "Hell has no fury and so on. Possible, but weak. La Montrose?" He listened intently and then said, "Stronger motive for her. And one that does include Alice. If Mrs. Montrose blamed Felix for her son's attempted suicide, she'd also blame his wife. What a rotten thing the Casparis did to those young lovers." Leaning forward, he thumped his glass down on the hearth. "How do you work Dolly Carter-White into this?"

"Her motive is even weaker than Nancy's. Dolly gave me to understand she was changing her mind about marrying Felix. What if it had been the reverse? Dolly is highly intelligent and seems to have a huge ego. Somehow I don't think she'd take kindly to having that ego bashed."

"Possible, but . . ." It was his turn to desert his chair and pace. Finally he swung around and spread his hands. "It simply won't work, Abigail. With the exception of Mrs. Montrose there's no earthly reason to harm Alice Caspari. And remember that boat and the telephone line. The only purpose for marooning us here must have been to finish off both the Casparis." He peered down at her. "You're holding something back."

"Something I hate to even contemplate." She bent her head.

The Black Knight stared down at her silver curls and then one word was wrung from him. *"Fran."*

"Fran Hornblower, who might once have been a girl named Blanche Waggoner."

"No."

"I feel exactly the same way." Miss Sanderson stared down at her folded hands. Fran of the warm, intelligent eyes, of the gentle capable hands, of the swift movements, and the rare compassion. She felt tears spring to her eyes and blinked them back. "Reggie, this is one time I'm *begging* you to poke holes in my reasoning."

Sinking cross-legged on the rug, he said somberly, "Give me your reasoning."

Miss Sanderson reported to him as she often had to Robert Forsythe. He listened as intently, interrupted twice, nodded once, and when she had finished, he said softly, "This emotion Fran felt when she spoke of David . . . it did seem genuine?"

"Heartbreakingly so. That wasn't faked. However, David could have been Sonny Montrose, and Lebanon, England. Reggie, two women were in that lorry accident in India where Blanche was supposed to have been killed. What if their identities were jumbled? What if Blanche came back as Fran Hornblower?"

"And years later took a backbreaking job on this island because Peggy Canard's daughter was a friend of Felix Caspari's." His golden fingers tore at the nap of the rug. "Why *years*? Why wait so long?"

"Fran doesn't seem a truly violent woman. Perhaps she fought back that hatred for years and then something happened to make it explode into murder." Miss Sanderson placed a hand on the young man's shoulder. "Reggie, three weeks ago the life supports were removed from Sonny Montrose and he was allowed to die."

White teeth nibbled at his lower lip. "It seems so . . . airtight. That description you were given of Blanche, it's sketchy, but it does fit Fran. Tall, thin, brown eyes and hair. Alice Caspair told you the girl was younger than she was. Alice was in her mid-forties. Fran must be in her late thirties. Damn it! That fits too." He moved restlessly. "And I can *see* Felix getting Fran to help him in the attic. She's kind of a servant and he had nothing but contempt for menials. Give them a few pounds and they'd do anything. Abigail, if anyone ever deserved a knife in the back, that bastard did. Let's forget this. If the police unmask Fran, all right. If they don't, let's keep our ruddy mouths shut. I happen to sympathize with this murderer."

She said wearily, "I'd like to agree, but we can't."

"*Justice*," he said scathingly.

"She has to be stopped. Reggie, who is responsible for Sonny Montrose's actual death?"

"Christ!"

"Sybil Clifton Montrose is the next one on Blanche Waggoner's list." She reached for her flash. "We'd better warn her."

"About Fran?"

"We've no real proof. We'll tell her of Alice's death and also tell her to keep her door locked and not to let anyone in."

It took some time to rouse the old woman. When she finally opened her door, the fine fluff of gray hair stood up like a ruff. But her eyes were alert and she pointed the tiny derringer, not at Miss Sanderson, but at the man beside her.

"I've been doing some thinking," she told them. "I'm not worried about you, Abigail, but that man is not entering my room."

Reggie tried to sound jovial. "Fine teatment for a knight."

"The proper treatment for a man with good reason to hate Felix. Now, what do you want? I'd just nicely dozed off when—"

Miss Sanderson took a step forward. "It's about Alice Caspari—"

163

"If she has her nose in the jenever again you can handle her." She started to close the door.

"Alice is dead," Reggie told her.

The derringer wavered and she clutched the door for support. The color drained from her face and she swayed. Reggie put out a hand and she stepped back, jerking up the weapon. "How?" she whispered.

"A knitting needle," Miss Sanderson said. "Thrust through her ear into her..." She pulled herself together. "For your safety you must keep your door locked and let no one in. In the morning I'll stop by for you. Understand? *No* one."

The gray head bobbed and the door shut. Reggie and Miss Sanderson heard a bolt being shot into position. Reggie jerked his head. "Better let Dolly know too."

Dolly took it better than the old woman had. She still wore her red jumpsuit, and behind her Miss Sanderson could see a table with a portable typewriter and piles of yellow sheets. On the dressing table the roses were shedding petals that looked like bright drops of blood. Dolly agreed it was a sound idea to keep her door locked, thanked them, and turned back to her worktable.

"Lucky devil," Reggie said. "At least she has something to keep her mind busy."

"Tomorrow," Miss Sanderson told him, "one of us has to be with Mrs. Montrose all the time."

"Or With Fran."

"Yes," she said brokenly. "Or with Fran Hornblower."

CHAPTER FOURTEEN

WHEN MISS SANDERSON ESCORTED MRS. MONTROSE into the kitchen for breakfast, they found most of the others already gathered. The only person missing was Fran. Reggie, a towel pinned around his narrow waist, was at the stove turning bacon in sizzling grease. Nancy was toasting bread, and Hielkje was laying the table. Perched side by side on tall stools, Gavin Lebonhom and Dolly watched.

"Where's Fran?" Miss Sanderson asked Hielkje.

"Lighting the fire in the saloon bar. She hasn't brought fuel in yet. Said you had the keys. But she said there should be enough coal to last until this afternoon." Setting down a plate, Hielkje rubbed a broad hand across her brow. "I don't know where Fran gets all the energy from. I feel like a wet rag."

Fran popped in from the saloon bar and gave Miss Sanderson a cheerful smile. "You've a smudge on your cheek," the secretary told her.

"But I've a song in my heart."

Gavin said peevishly, "You're perkier than you were last night."

"With good reason." Fran cocked her head. "Hear anything?"

165

He listened and then said, "Nothing."

"And that's the answer." Striding over to a window, she pulled back cotton curtains. Weak sunlight streamed into the room. "Early this morning the storm blew itself out."

"Thank God!" Dolly sagged on the stool. "The causeway?"

"I'll have to wait for low tide." Fran pushed up a sleeve and consulted her watch. "Four hours, give or take a few minutes."

With knees that felt like jelly and a pounding heart, Miss Sanderson dropped onto the nearest chair. Reggie cracked an egg and deftly dropped it into bacon grease. "You all right, Abigail?"

Unable to speak, she merely jerked her head. Fran glanced around. "Any volunteers to go with me?" She turned to the Black Knight. "How about you?"

"Uh-huh. One stint I never put in was that of a tight-rope walker. I'm afraid it's up to you."

Everyone started to talk at once, but Miss Sanderson moodily watched Reggie. She knew why he hadn't offered to go with Fran. The Black Knight was hoping she would make a run for it. Miss Sanderson found she was hoping the same thing. Take a car, she told Fran silently, get away from here and never let yourself be found. In the meantime . . . Reggie lowered a hot platter of bacon and eggs on the table and the sight and smell made her stomach lurch. She reached for a slice of toast.

Hielkje, as usual, had a hearty meal, but as soon as her plate was emptied, she got to her feet. "You'll have to make do without me—"

"As soon as this business is settled," Gavin growled, "I'm going to make do without you permanently."

"I don't care! Fire me if you want. I . . . I can't stand any more. I'm going up and lock myself in and take one of those pills Dr. Parker gave me."

Fran called after her, "Make sure that's only one pill." She smiled at Miss Sanderson. "Hielkje has a tendency to overdo medication. Waits until she gets a cold and then gulps half a bottle of vitamin capsules."

"She's still on the right track." Dolly stretched her long frame like a cat. "Jester or no Jester, I've a deadline to make, and I'm going to barricade myself in my room until the police get here."

Mrs. Montrose hesitated and then scooped up her cat. "Sounds like a good idea."

"I think," Miss Sanderson said quickly, "you should stay here. It's safer."

"I'm quite able to know where I'll be safest." Her black monkey eyes gleamed. "I suppose most of us have ways of calming our nerves. Poor Alice always knitted and I read Austen. Right at present I'm rereading *Emma* and I find it most relaxing. I'll take along this last rasher for Omar. He's wild for bacon." The huge cat reached out a paw and she scolded, "Naughty boy. When we get to our room mama will break it up for you."

The next one to rise was Gavin. He told them expansively, "Going to get all the facts down while they're still fresh."

"Facts?" Fran's dark brows pulled together. "You mean about the murders?"

"Of course. I've made notes on Felix's and now must fill in Alice's death. There's a book here, you know. Possible best-seller." Jauntily, he made his departure.

"Not if you write it," Fran muttered. She said quickly, "Forgot you were still here, Nancy. Spoke out of turn."

"I happen to agree with you. I've always known Gavin is simply dreaming about being a writer." Taking Miss Sanderson's hand, the girl squeezed it. "Auntie Abby, I'm sorry I said those horrible things to you yesterday. When I found Alice—" Nancy gulped and flung both arms around the older woman's neck. "I knew then what you were trying to do. Trying to stop things like that from happening and doing it all alone. You're not cold, you're very brave."

"I didn't prevent Alice's death."

"You tried. And if you were gentle and soft like Mother, you couldn't do things like that." Honey curls brushed softly against Miss Sanderson's cheeks and the girl whispered, "I'm sorry I disappointed you."

Holding the girl away from her, Miss Sanderson gazed down into the hazel eyes. "Nancy, I'm sorry too. Sorry I confused you with your mother. You do look like her, but you're Nancy, she was Peggy. I can never really understand your world, any more than you can mine, but surely we can try. We can be friends."

"We can, Auntie Abby." Nancy, her face radiant, stepped back. "I'm going up to Gavin now. Try to make amends to him for what I said yesterday."

Reggie was mopping grease off the stove. He said disgustedly, "Rats deserting the sinking kitchen. I'm going to have dishpan hands. Fran, how about grabbing a towel?"

She laughed. "The Black Knight's fans should see him now! It's my turn to say sorry. Must be catching. You and Abigail will have to cope. I'm off on fuel detail. Abigail, I'll need the keys."

Reggie shot a look at Miss Sanderson and she said firmly, "Both fuel and washing up can wait. Fran, while you're gone this afternoon, Reggie and I will handle the coal. I vote the three of us take a holiday."

"And I second the motion. " Pulling off his improvised apron, Reggie threw it on the counter. "You two make yourselves comfortable in the saloon bar and I'll bring coffee."

Miss Sanderson took the younger woman's arm and led her into the next room. It was as warm as the kitchen, with a fire blazing on the grate and two heaters beaming warmth. They had barely taken chairs when Reggie wheeled in a metal serving wagon. A wheel squeaked dismally. "Handy things, these wagons," Reggie said.

Jumping up, Fran bent over a front wheel. "In some ways, but . . ." She spun the wheel and it squeaked again. "The wheels on these ruddy carts always need oiling. Well, that can wait too. Anyone care for a touch of brandy with their coffee?"

"Fine idea," Reggie said. "I'll get it."

Fran glanced after him. "That lad missed his calling. He'd have made a dandy butler."

Reggie came trotting back and extended the bottle. Both the women nodded and he titled it over their cups. Leaning back, Fran asked, "I understand you told La Montrose and Dolly about Alice last night. How did they take it?"

"Nothing seems to ruffle our romance writer." Pushing the footstool over, Reggie sat down between them. "It hit Mrs. Montrose hard. She positively blanched, and I thought she was going to pass out." He pointed at the picture over the mantel. "Noel Canard wasn't quite as grisly in that one. Noticed it yesterday."

Fran looked up. "Nancy said her mother told her that was one of Noel's earlier works, painted shortly after Peggy and he came to live here. Maybe he wasn't so morbid then."

"Have you looked at it, Abigail?" Reggie asked.

"No. I've had quite enough of Noel Canard."

"Take a look. You're going to be pleasantly surprised."

Miss Sanderson put down her cup and rose. Reggie was right. This watercolor was fairly mild. It pictured only one child, a towheaded boy who looked around eight. He was forlornly squinting down at his feet. Half buried in the grass was a pair of wire-rimmed glasses. Both lenses were shattered. "For Noel this is almost poetic," she remarked. "All I can see is a little chap, terribly shortsighted, who has broken his glasses and will have to find his way home without them."

Fran nodded. "Nary a monster in sight. Not even a cliff the boy might fall off. The only mishap I can see is that he's thumping a shoulder against that tree."

Sliding back in her chair, Miss Sanderson rested her head against the back of it and closed her eyes. As though from a distance she could hear Reggie's voice, sounding determinedly cheerful, and Fran's, sounding quite naturally cheerful. Reggie was asking Fran if she planned to stay on at the inn, and she was telling him she never made plans, simply went with the tide. Fran, go with the tide, Miss Sanderson silently urged. We'll keep Mrs. Montrose safe and you get across that causeway and disappear. She wondered how Robby would feel about her emotional involvement with this murderer and then found she didn't care. For the first time in days she relaxed, allowing her mind to wander aimlessly. That weary mind fell effortlessly into a light sleep and no nightmare disturbed it. The dream that formed was only puzzling. She watched a chubby boy, squinting with myopic eyes and rolling a serving wagon along that had a squeaky wheel. The boy lurched into a doorjamb and banged his shoulder. Something fell, and at first the dreamer thought it was the child's broken glasses. Then she saw it was an ornate emerald pendant.

Shaking her head from side to side, Miss Sanderson roused. Blearily, she saw Reggie and Fran staring at her. "Napping?" Reggie said. "You were mumbling something about a cart."

Miss Sanderson didn't reply. She jerked up, her thumbnail drumming against a front tooth. Reggie started to speak, but Fran shushed him. Both of them stared at the secretary. Her hand fell away from her mouth and she pointed. "Fran, what do you always call that?"

"A serving cart. Abigail, are you all right?"

Miss Sanderson was on her feet. "Dear God! I've been a blind fool. As blind as that—" She waved toward the painting and then she was running. When she reached the foyer, she found Reggie and Fran were pounding along behind her.

"Wait," Reggie called. "Where in hell are you going?"

"To keep Mrs. Montrose alive."

Fran gasped, "She's locked in. She won't let anyone in."

Miss Sanderson tore open the door to the guest wing. "There's one person she'd open that door for."

They raced past closed doors. Dolly's, the one that Alice Caspari had slept in, the Black Knight's. Miss Sanderson thudded to a stop. She flung open the door of Mrs. Montrose's room and then stretched out an arm to halt Reggie and Fran.

Sunlight streamed through the window, highlighting the simian face of the professional hostess. Mrs. Montrose sat stiffly, a hand on each bony knee. Beside her a tall woman stood. A hand bearing an opal ring held a tiny derringer. Sunlight sparkled from the inlaid handle. The muzzle was jammed against Mrs. Montrose's fluffy head.

Creamy hair brushed the younger woman's shoulders as she turned an oval face in their direction. From the face of Barbie Doll, the dark brown eyes of Blanche Waggoner regarded them.

CHAPTER FIFTEEN

For moments all that could be heard was the hiss of coal on the grate, a deep intake of breath from behind Miss Sanderson, and Omar's ragged purr from the rug near Reggie's feet.

Blanche's voice broke the silence. She squinted and asked, "Who is that behind you, Abigail?"

"Fran and Reggie. It's all over, Blanche. Put down that toy."

"As Sybil Montrose told us, this is not a toy. Granted, there's only one bullet, but that will be enough. If one of you move, she's dead. That I can see enough to do."

"Contacts," Fran whispered. "Green contacts."

"I used to wear glasses, but Rory decided they didn't fit my glamorous new image. When I had my hair bleached, he insisted on green contacts. They've come in handy. Mrs. Montrose never guessed my identity. Not until I took them out so she could recognize me."

Mrs. Montrose said in a monotone, "I knew her *then*. I never forgot those eyes. She was the one person I didn't fear. When she tapped on my door, I was...I was so happy to see her."

"And I was happy to see you alone." Blanche smiled

down at the old woman. "Happy to talk with you before I send you to join the Casparis in hell." She peered at Miss Sanderson. "I saved her until last. Of the three, she was the most important to me. You know, legal secretary, I'm curious. I would have been afraid of Forsythe, but I didn't think you could figure this puzzle out."

"A few moments ago the pieces fell into position. Fran always calls those serving wagons *carts*. Reggie said when we told Mrs. Montrose about Alice's death, she positively *blanched*. And he meant she went *white*. Then I remembered that silly business about names the second day we were in this place, and I realized that Blanche Waggoner was now Dolly Carter-White. I also remembered that Blanche wore 'granny glasses.'"

The blond head bobbed. "And doubtless you recalled my bunting you all over the hall the other night when I was going to the bath. I'd taken out my contacts, and although I managed to keep my face in shadow, I couldn't see properly. It would appear, Abigail, that you're a sleuth!"

"And a realist. There's no use in harming Mrs. Montrose. Fran and Reggie and I will have no problem holding you for the police."

A dreadful smile touched the tinted lips. "You work with a barrister. Tell me, will my sentence be any longer for three murders than for two?" Mrs. Montrose moaned and Blanche glanced down at her. "Don't make me impatient. The old value life, and if Abigail can keep me talking, you'll have a few more precious moments. Anyway, I want to tell you how I did it and why—"

"I know why," Mrs. Montrose whispered. "You're *mad*."

"She's not mad," Fran said evenly. "She's coldly, horribly sane."

"And you should have been a doctor," Blanche said mockingly. "Now, Abigail, try to stall me with questions."

"I have no questions. I know how you became Maud Epstein. She was the woman killed in the the lorry accident. Your IDs must have become mixed, and you decided it was a good idea to change your identity—"

"Wrong. I'd taken out an insurance policy and made Maud the beneficiary. I'd no one else to put down for that, and I was fond of her. Maud had no one waiting in England for her either, so I simply let them think it was Blanche Waggoner who had died so I could collect the money. After all, it was *mine*. I'd paid the premiums. I'm not a thief!"

A moot point, Miss Sanderson thought numbly. This woman had killed two people and was holding a gun to a third and was worried that her honesty might be in question. "Did you come back to England to take your revenge on—"

"No, I'll admit I still hated the three of them. Felix and Alice and Mrs. Montrose had taken Sonny away from me, ruined his life and my own, but he was still alive and . . ." Blanche's voice trailed off and she stared down at the top of Sybil Montrose's head. "That was why I started to write romances. Critics claim that although my plots differ, the hero and heroine always remain the same. They're correct about that. Sonny was always the strong, stalwart hero, and I was always the beautiful heroine. You see, as long as he was alive, there was hope we'd find *our* happy ending and—"

"My son was *not* alive," Mrs. Montrose rasped. "After he shot himself he was only medically—"

"Shut up, you old fool!" Blanche dug the barrel of the tiny gun into gray hair. "Look at the advances in modern science. There was still a chance for a miracle, that Sonny would be cured—"

"No!" Mrs. Montrose's voice rang out. "His brain was destroyed. He was only a shell—"

"Be quiet!" Miss Sanderson ordered. The older

woman's life hung by a thread and she seemed to be deliberately goading Blanche. She said hastily, "When you went to Venice, did you plan to meet Felix?"

"It happened exactly as I told you." Blanche laughed. "I couldn't believe it. I thought Felix would surely recognize me, might even remember my voice, but I'd changed too much. He was obviously infatuated, and although I loathed him I played along. It amused me and I decided to play a joke on the joker. After he divorced his faithful Alice and announced our engagement, I planned to break it off, as publicly and messily as I could, and then tell him who I actually was." The laughter faded and the oval face became blank again. "Three weeks ago Mrs. Montrose won her court case and Sonny...she *murdered* him. I knew I'd never write again. With Sonny dead there was nothing left —no warmth, no passion, no dreams."

"And you came here for revenge."

"Yes. You see, they'd taken Sonny away from me, my writing away from me. Oh, I pretended I was writing, but I knew I'd never write again. There was nothing left for me but this. And it was so easy. Last evening, Abigail, I lied to you. Felix believed I enjoyed his jokes. He asked me to help him with the joke he planned to play on Gavin. After he read Gavin's script, he came to me and I agreed to help. That night I went down to the boathouse and put an axe through the boat's bottom."

"And the next day you cut the telephone cord while the rest of us were in the dining room." Miss Sanderson touched Reggie's arm and pointed down. He followed her eyes and gave a small nod. "Did you tell Felix your identity before—"

"Of course. I would have liked to have done it the same way as I did with Alice, face-to-face, looking into his eyes. But Felix was too big and powerful for that, so I had to wait until he'd arranged himself on the dumbwaiter. Before

I drove that knife into his back, I told him. Now, my dear Mrs. Montrose, time for you to follow those lovely friends of yours. Do say hello to Felix and Alice for me."

Now or never, Miss Sanderson thought, and she ran into the room. Blanche whirled, automatically twisting the derringer away from the old woman. Its barrel pointed at the secretary. At the same moment, Reggie stooped, seized the cat, and hurled it at Blanche. Omar landed on her arm. He hissed with fury and raked her flesh with talonlike claws.

Fran leapt past Miss Sanderson and grappled with Blanche. The derringer gave a tinny little bark and the secretary staggered back. It's true, she thought, you feel the bullet before you hear the sound.

She was aware that Mrs. Montrose, with remarkable speed, was heading to shelter behind the bed. Reggie was helping Fran Hornblower, and they were tying Blanche to the desk chair. It looked as though they were using tights as ropes.

Miss Sanderson lost interest. She slid down and braced her back against the wall. The wall felt cold, but something warm was welling from her upper body. I'm bleeding to death, she thought drearily. Abigail Sanderson's first case is her last one. Now I'll never see Robby's face when he opens his jade tree at Christmas.

Reggie was shouting, and then Fran was kneeling beside the secretary. "Get the first-aid box," she told the singer. "Under the desk in the lobby. Hurry!"

"I'm dying," Miss Sanderson said without much interest.

Gentle capable hands were cutting Miss Sanderson's sweater away from a shoulder. "Like hell you are," Fran said inelegantly. "One of those flesh wounds you read about in thrillers. Painful but certainly not fatal." She said over her shoulder, "Stop wringing your hands, Reggie, and make tea. Strong, and throw in lots of sugar."

Mrs. Montrose had retrieved her cat and was joyously hugging him. "Good Omar," she told the animal. "You saved your mama's life!"

Fran grinned wryly at Miss Sanderson. "How does it feel to join the club? That's the gratitude crusaders generally get. *You* get the pain, and the ruddy *cat* gets the hero badge."

She pressed a bandage against the wound. Miss Sanderson got the pain and promptly passed out.

CHAPTER SIXTEEN

THERE WERE TIMES WHEN ROBERT FORSYTHE WONdered why he kept his rambling costly home in Sussex. Tonight, as he looked around his study, he knew. Meeks had kindled a wood fire, and the smell of fruit wood mingled pleasantly with that of pine needles. On the Aubusson carpet near the desk used by generations of Forsythes was the tree erected for his private enjoyment. The tall tree in the drawing room easily outshone this one both in size and decoration. The baubles on his study tree showed their age, gilt flaking from fragile glass, an angel at the top with a mended wing, a bluebird missing most of its tail feathers. But each shabby object represented a memory, a moment that would never come again.

Reaching out, he gently touched a small object. "You brought this for me on my fifth Christmas," he told his companion.

"Frosty the Snowman? That happened to be your fourth Christmas. The same year that your father gave you the electric train."

"Right. I was recovering from measles—"

"Whooping cough," Miss Sanderson corrected.

He turned to look at her. "Sure you're not too tired?"

She shook her silver curls. "We always see Christmas day arrive, Robby." She glanced up at the mantel clock. "Not long now. The evening went well, didn't it?"

"Enjoyed by all. And your new image proved to be a sensation. Colonel Barton was practically goggling at you. Better watch it. He's shopping around for a third wife."

"Some of the guests found the sling intriguing. Inspired idea to use silk to match my dress."

He glanced at the green sling that did match the final layer of chiffon and turned away. The shock of that telephone call from Inspector James of the Finchley police force was still too recent, too harrowing. He said gruffly, "Sandy, that was the stupidest move you ever made."

"How did I know a murder party was going to turn into the real thing?"

"You know what I mean. Walking right into a gun!"

"Only a derringer, Robby, and I didn't think the woman could see well enough to even hit the wall. Anyway, I was only trying to distract her." She squirmed into a more comfortable position and changed the subject. "Bubbly ready yet?"

The cooler sat on his desk and he turned the long-necked bottle. "Just about there. But you get only one glass. I noticed the amount of punch you were downing."

"Four cups, but who was counting. Aren't you curious about who rang me up?"

"I know. Mrs. Meeks told me it was the Black Knight. She was all aflutter. Believe it or not, but she adores him, says she has all his records. When you came back, you looked like a cat full of cream. Good news?"

"Excellent. Nancy Lebonhom is finally convinced that her father, dead or alive, does not roam the Jester, and Gavin and she are keeping it on. Mrs. Montrose, who seems as canny about money as my Aggie, is funding the rest of the renovations and paying for central heating and so on."

"Ye gods! They're going to continue giving parties after having two murders and an attempted third enlivening their first?"

Lifting shapely legs onto a hassock, Miss Sanderson grinned impishly up at him. "I understand Gavin has written that plot into a new play. I wonder who will play my role? Reggie says the Lebonhoms and Mrs. Montrose think they have a gold mine on that island."

"No doubt they have. I wonder whether they plan to have a ghost in a black mask wafting down the corridors?" He bent and poked at a log, and orange and red fire devils spiraled up. "I overheard part of your conversation with Gene Emory, Sandy. Something about having already made your New Year's resolutions."

"Two resolutions, and don't look so dubious. These I intend to keep. Number one—never ever again will Abigail Sanderson accept a second case, and—"

"You certainly proved your ability on this one!"

"And found out exactly how glamorous it is to carry the full detecting load. From now on, you're the detective, and I'll happily bumble along making notes and asking asinine questions."

He shook his head. "On that one I'll wait and see. What's your second resolution?"

Her sound arm made a sweeping gesture, starting at the cap of metallic curls, wafting down the chiffon dress, and pointing at the extravagant emerald shoes. "All this goes."

He cocked his head and looked down at her. "I'll admit I wouldn't mind seeing your hair back to normal, and those heels are treacherous, but Sandy, do hang on to that dress."

Her eyes narrowed. "You're up to something."

How, Forsythe thought, do you try to conceal something from a person who remembers you had whooping cough on your fourth Christmas? It was his turn to hastily change the subject. "Did the Black Knight have any other tidings of joy?"

She was diverted and her eyes sparkled. "That was what made me so happy. Fran is leaving the Jester for good. As soon as Gavin got back to normal, he fired Hielkje and—"

"Where is Fran going?"

"If you give me a chance, I'll tell you. Reggie Knight has decided to do something constructive about his brother's memory. He's investing in a small nursing home near Finchley, and Fran Hornblower is going to manage it. It's to be called the Damien Day Home."

"And the ailing cook?"

"Hielkje goes with Fran. In what capacity I don't know."

"From what you said about Hielkje Visser, my guess would be as resident patient." He glanced at the clock. "Uh-oh, time for champagne and present opening."

He hurried over to the tree and carefully detached two presents. They were small, one wrapped in red paper, the other in silver. The red one had a silver bow, the other a large green bow. Under the opulent tree in the drawing room were mounds of gaily wrapped gifts, but opening their special gifts to each other had become a tradition. Always in the study, always alone. As he handed the silver package to Miss Sanderson, the clock majestically struck midnight.

"Merry Christmas, Sandy." He kissed her brow and she smiled up at him.

"Merry Christmas, Robby. You open yours first."

"You go first."

"Let's do it at the same time!"

Paper and ribbons and bows flew, and Miss Sanderson held up an emerald pendant set into antique gold. "Robby," she whispered.

181

He was staring down at the tiny jade tree. "I can hear the bird singing," he said rapturously.

"So could I. I heard it in the shop."

Carefully, he carried the tree to his desk, situated it dead center, covered it with the glass domed lid from a candy dish. Then he took the pendant Miss Sanderson was extending and clasped it around her neck. Standing back, he beamed. "I *knew* it would look wonderful with that dress." His secretary's eyes were moist and he said huskily, "One glass of bubbly and I'm bundling you off to bed. Big day tomorrow. Sixteen dinner guests, crackling goose, plum pudding, and . . ."

He pulled the cork and poured. Handing a glass to Miss Sanderson, he knelt at her side. "To Christmas past, Sandy."

"And to many more to come."

"Amen." Robert Forsythe touched his glass to hers and they both drank.

ABOUT THE AUTHOR

E.X. Giroux lives in Surrey, British Columbia.

DEADLY MYSTERIES

and only
Robert Forsythe
knows who-dunnit!

Stories by E.X. Giroux